W9-DCB-219

"I Dare You...."

Scott's dark brown eyes met hers in a nonverbal challenge. "I dare you to go out with me, to see past the flashbulbs and gossip-sheet rumors about me."

Raine wanted to accept. It would give her a chance to put her idea of making *him* fall for *her* into action. But was she willing to risk her job just so she could one-up him? And she definitely was going to one-up this man.

"What's the matter? Scared you can't handle me off the set, where you're not in charge?" he asked in that silky tone of his.

She raised her chin. "I'm not scared of any man."

Scott stepped closer, his body a mere whisper away from hers. "Then I'll pick you up in your suite at eight." His breath tingled on her skin. "Be prepared for the night of your life."

Dear Reader,

Thanks for taking time out of your hectic life to pick up and enjoy a Silhouette Desire novel. We have six outstanding reads for you this month, beginning with the latest in our continuity series, THE ELLIOTTS. Anna DePalo's *Cause for Scandal* will thrill you with a story of a quiet twin who takes on her identical sister's persona and falls for a dynamic hero. Look for her sister to turn the tables next month.

The fabulous Kathie DeNosky wraps up her ILLEGITIMATE HEIRS trilogy with the not-to-be-missed *Betrothed for the Baby*—a compelling engagement-of-convenience story. We welcome back Mary Lynn Baxter to Silhouette Desire with *Totally Texan,* a sensual story with a Lone Star hero to drool over. WHAT HAPPENS IN VEGAS...is perhaps better left there unless you're the heroine of Katherine Garbera's *Her High-Stakes Affair*—she's about to make the biggest romantic wager of all.

Also this month are two stories of complex relationships. Cathleen Galitz's *A Splendid Obsession* delves into the romance between an ex-model with a tormented past and the hero who finds her all the inspiration he needs. And Nalini Singh's *Secrets in the Marriage Bed* finds a couple on the brink of separation with a reason to fight for their marriage thanks to a surprise pregnancy.

Here's hoping this month's selection of Silhouette Desire novels bring you all the enjoyment you crave.

Happy reading!

Melissa Jeglinski

Melissa Jeglinski
Senior Editor
Silhouette Desire

Please address questions and book requests to:
Silhouette Reader Service
U.S.: 3010 Walden Ave., P.O. Box 1325, Buffalo, NY 14269
Canadian: P.O. Box 609, Fort Erie, Ont. L2A 5X3

KATHERINE GARBERA

Her High-Stakes Affair

Published by Silhouette Books
America's Publisher of Contemporary Romance

If you purchased this book without a cover you should be aware that this book is stolen property. It was reported as "unsold and destroyed" to the publisher, and neither the author nor the publisher has received any payment for this "stripped book."

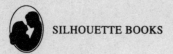

SILHOUETTE BOOKS

RECYCLED PAPER · RECYCLED PAPER

ISBN 0-373-76714-5

HER HIGH-STAKES AFFAIR

Copyright © 2006 by Katherine Garbera

All rights reserved. Except for use in any review, the reproduction or utilization of this work in whole or in part in any form by any electronic, mechanical or other means, now known or hereafter invented, including xerography, photocopying and recording, or in any information storage or retrieval system, is forbidden without the written permission of the editorial office, Silhouette Books, 233 Broadway, New York, NY 10279 U.S.A.

All characters in this book have no existence outside the imagination of the author and have no relation whatsoever to anyone bearing the same name or names. They are not even distantly inspired by any individual known or unknown to the author, and all incidents are pure invention.

This edition published by arrangement with Harlequin Books S.A.

® and TM are trademarks of Harlequin Books S.A., used under license. Trademarks indicated with ® are registered in the United States Patent and Trademark Office, the Canadian Trade Marks Office and in other countries.

Visit Silhouette Books at www.eHarlequin.com

Printed in U.S.A.

Books by Katherine Garbera

Silhouette Desire

The Bachelor Next Door #1104
Miranda's Outlaw #1169
Her Baby's Father #1289
Overnight Cinderella #1348
Baby at His Door #1367
Some Kind of Incredible #1395
The Tycoon's Temptation #1414
The Tycoon's Lady #1464
Cinderella's Convenient Husband #1466
Tycoon for Auction #1504
Cinderella's Millionaire #1520
In Bed with Beauty #1535
Cinderella's Christmas Affair #1546
Let It Ride #1558
Sin City Wedding #1567
Mistress Minded #1587
Rock Me All Night #1672
†*His Wedding-Night Wager* #1708
†*Her High-Stakes Affair* #1714

Silhouette Bombshell

Exposed #10
Night Life #23
The Amazon Strain #43

*King of Hearts
†What Happens in Vegas…

KATHERINE GARBERA

took one brief trip to Las Vegas and was hooked with endless story ideas and a fascination with that playground known as Sin City. She's written more than twenty books and has been nominated for *Romantic Times BOOKClub*'s career achievement awards in Series Fantasy and Series Adventure. Katherine recently moved to the Dallas area where she lives with her husband and their two children. Visit Katherine on the Web at www.katherinegarbera.com.

This book is dedicated to my kids,
Courtney and Lucas, who keep me on my toes
and make every day an adventure!

One

"Hey, sexy lady. Where do you want me today?"

Raine Montgomery bit the inside of her cheek not to respond to Scott Rivers. Every morning it was the same line or some variation of it. It should have sounded like a pickup line but didn't. Instead he made her want to believe she was a sexy lady, even though she'd had enough experience with gamblers to know they never told the truth.

"Can't decide?" he asked, slipping an arm around her waist.

She stepped away from him. "In your chair at the table."

"Honey, when are you going to loosen up with me?"

"When you stop flirting with every woman who walks by."

"Is it making you jealous?"

"No."

Scott laughed and walked away from her as the other players trickled in.

She'd gotten into the film business for one reason and one reason only. She'd dreamed of the moment when she'd be called onstage at the Academy Awards to accept her Oscar for best director. She even had her speech rehearsed:

"I'd like to thank the Academy for recognizing my accomplishments, and I'd like the rest of the world to know that Missy Talbot is a spoiled bitch and my dad isn't a loser."

Okay, so it was a little melodramatic, but she'd been in junior high at the time and it had seemed like the perfect solution to her dismal and dreary life in New Jersey.

But her dream hadn't gotten her to the Oscars; in fact, she wasn't even close to winning a People's Choice Award or even an MTV one. She doubted anyone was going to be giving her an award for World Champion Celebrity Poker Showdown.

The taping ran for four weeks, with three celebrities and three champions from across the country who competed. In each week's episode two games were played and at the end of the show two players were eliminated. When just two players remained, they played two high-stakes games to determine the celebrity poker champ.

The show was essentially a high-stakes Texas hold 'em poker game where viewers could log on to a Web site and win prizes by correctly guessing if the celebrity winner had been bluffing or really held the cards needed to win.

Spawned in part by the reality craze that was sweeping through the television industry, the show tapped into the public's desire to watch celebrities spend their money and their free time. Every four weeks a new group of celebrities and champs were brought in. Then at the end of the season they had a winners-only play-off.

Their show taped a month's worth of episodes in one week. Each person on the show signed a waiver promising not to reveal the results, because viewers had the chance to vote on who they thought was the best and win a myriad of prizes that had been donated by sponsors. The celebrities were playing for charities as were the champions.

Raine had given all the players a wide berth because her producer, Joel Tanner, didn't like her or any of the crew mingling with the players. In fact there was a clear no-fraternization clause in the contracts signed by everyone on the set, both in front of the camera and behind the scenes. Joel wanted to make sure they didn't end up with any kind of lawsuit because of the way the players were shown.

Prizes were given to viewers who chose the winner each week. So how Raine shot and edited the show could influence them. They'd had to fire a cameraman last season because he'd been involved with one of the players and had been giving her more camera time than the other players.

This set of shows was being taped in the exclusive Chimera Casino on the strip in Las Vegas. Still, it was hard work, and Raine rubbed the back of her neck as she headed toward the director's booth. Some people called it the God booth because her voice could be heard but she couldn't be seen. Yet Raine knew she was as far from God as any person could be.

Especially since right now she was having impure thoughts about actor Scott Rivers. She entered the booth and put on her headphones. Since all of the players were miked, she could hear their small talk. The deep sexy tones of Scott's voice came over her headphones and she paused to listen. He was the first guy she'd ever been tempted to break her contract for, and she really struggled to keep resisting him every day. She wished he'd lose…. No, that wasn't true. She knew enough about men to realize that sooner or later he'd stop asking her out, and she honestly wanted to enjoy flirting with him until that happened.

"Shot down again, eh, stud?"

Scott glanced over at Stevie Taylor, the notoriously debauched lead singer for Viper, a heavy-metal band that had been on the cutting edge of music fifteen years ago. Instead of being a has-been, Stevie had the kind of talent and energy that had kept him in the mainstream. He simply changed his style to fit the younger audiences' tastes.

That being said, the man was an ass sometimes, and Scott suspected Stevie was still pissed off about losing to him at the PGA celebrity golf tournament last month in Hawaii. Or maybe it was the fact that Scott had unwittingly been the object of Stevie's third wife's affection.

"Some women take more time than others," Scott said. Especially women like Raine Montgomery. Not that Raine fit into a box or a category. In fact, he knew she'd be ticked off that he'd even thought of putting her in one. "They aren't all impressed with long hair and fast cars."

"I guess that means you have to try harder," Stevie said.

There was an edge to his voice that Scott chose to ignore. Every day was work for Scott. He'd grown up on a soundstage and had learned early on to act the way others found acceptable. With Stevie he acted like a babe magnet always on the prowl, because that was what the legendary rock front-man understood. With Raine he acted…hell, he wasn't doing such a great job of acting with Raine. She made him forget he was playing a role.

"Sure. Everything worth having takes some effort." And Raine was definitely worth the effort. Worth even this job. Not that he was too concerned about getting fired. The producer was a good friend of his, and they went back a long way. He wondered how Raine felt about the no-fraternization clause they'd both signed.

Scott was honest enough to admit that the gambler in him wanted to take a chance on it. The added risk increased the odds that she wouldn't go out with him unless she really wanted to. He couldn't explain it beyond that but knew himself well enough by now to know that there was something appealing about the idea.

"You're working up a sweat and she's barely noticing you, Rivers. What would your fan club say?"

Scott didn't respond to the goad. He didn't have a fan club and Stevie knew it. His child stardom had translated into cult-classic films in his early twenties and two one-offs that had turned into blockbusters. He acted when he felt like it, preferring to spend most of his time working with the charitable trust he had set up with his own money. "I'm not worried, Stevie."

"Some boys aren't meant to play in the big leagues," the other man said.

"Whatever. You know she can't really show that she's attracted to me."

"Because she isn't?" Stevie said with a snicker.

"Because we work together." A man like Stevie would never understand the distinction, but Scott knew that Raine would. That her job and her reputation would be important to her. He understood why.

"I wouldn't let that stop me."

He wasn't going to defend himself like some teenage boy with his first woman. Scott was thirty-eight, and he couldn't believe he'd allowed himself to get drawn into this conversation.

He'd arrived early on the set hoping for some alone time with Raine, and he'd gotten it. He just hadn't expected Stevie to show up.

"What, no glib remark?"

"You're an ass, you know that?"

Stevie laughed. "You're not the first to say it. But that doesn't change the fact that Ms. Montgomery isn't exactly falling for you."

Stevie wasn't going to let this go. No matter what Scott said or did, Stevie was always going to bring up Raine. And Scott didn't want that.

"What would it take for you to drop this?"

"Prove me wrong. Prove you're not out of your element with Raine."

"How am I supposed to do that?"

"How about a little wager?"

"On a woman? Have you been living under a rock for the past twenty years?"

"There's no reason anyone other than the two of us has to know about it."

Famous last words. He glanced around the set. They appeared to be all alone, and so he thought they had the kind of privacy that was something of a luxury on a busy television or movie set.

"What'd you have in mind?"

"A simple bet…you get her in bed before the show wraps."

Scott had that tingling at the back of his neck that he always got before he did something risky. Like sky surfing or kayaking down dangerous rapids. Something that all of his self-preservation instincts said not to do. But he wanted Raine, and he suspected she wanted him, too.

He knew he'd never tell Stevie a single detail of his

time with her, but if it got Stevie off his back, then it might be worth it.

"What's the wager?"

"Fifty thousand."

"You're on."

Raine couldn't believe she'd just overheard Scott making a bet about her with Stevie Taylor. The rocker was as legendary for his kinky sex-capades as he was for his wicked guitar licks.

Why had she activated the microphones when she'd gotten into her booth? Because she was an idiot. This is what happens when you eavesdrop, she told herself.

Raine's hands shook, and she wanted to smack Scott right between the eyes. What the hell was he thinking making a bet about taking her to bed? That was low and mean. And it hurt so much because she'd thought he was different.

She leaned toward the booth's tinted window and glanced down at the floor where the two men stood away from everyone else.

Raine watched both men take their seats at the table and went back to her monitor to watch the screen. But all she saw was red. Having been the pawn in a gambler's game before, she refused to let it happen again.

She wasn't sure how to get the upper hand on Scott. As a child star, he'd grown up in front of America and had charmed everyone by coming into their homes once a week for fifteen years. In the three days they'd been in Vegas, Raine had yet to see one person deny the man anything he asked for—except her.

He was good-looking. Well, only if you liked guys with unruly hair that fell to their shoulders and who wore a goatee. Which, of course, she did.

And she'd been thinking that maybe it was time to take a chance again on a guy before she'd heard his bet. A bet about her. She wanted to sink to the floor and wrap her arms around her waist. But she didn't; instead she pressed the button so that the cast and crew could hear her.

"Places, please."

She hated that she was attracted to a man who seemed to bluff his way through life. She'd been raised by the ultimate con man. A grifter, bar none, who'd blended perfectly into any situation much the same way Scott seemed to. She knew that was what Scott was doing because no one could predict when he was bluffing or really holding a winning hand.

"Action."

She watched him playing his game, the ultimate con man in his environment. His words played over and over in her head. Fifty thousand dollars—that was what she was worth to him. She wished that she could get back at him, do something he wouldn't expect. Maybe run a con on him. Convince him she was falling for him. No one knew how to run a scam like a Montgomery.

And though she'd vowed to never again lie or betray anyone's confidence, it somehow seemed right to her that she do it now. With this man. The one she'd hoped might be different.

"Camera Two, you're out of focus. Camera One, pan the entire table like we discussed."

Raine stopped thinking about Scott and focused instead on her job. If she went through with this scam, there was a good chance she'd be putting her job on the line. Joel wouldn't forgive her if she broke his rules.

"And cut," she said, as the hand was dealt to everyone.

"No one move. Latesha, there's a shine coming off Stevie's forehead. Move Camera One to the left of the table and get ready to resume play."

The East Coast champ, Laurie Andrews, lifted her free hand. "I need a drink of water."

One of the production assistants got her a bottle of Evian and then disappeared out of scene. Raine called action and finished shooting the hand.

So far Scott had fooled them every time. He didn't have any of the "tells," the little signs that the other players had.

She left her booth and went back on the floor to find Andy, her assistant director. He was talking to the NASCAR driver—probably about cars. Andy had a thing about fast cars that bordered on obsession.

She signaled to him that she needed a word and stood a little to the side of everyone else. Scott glanced up from the food table and caught her staring at him. He arched one eyebrow at her in a very arrogant way that made her want to do something really immature like kick his shins.

Her nature was contrary, so she couldn't budge even when he pushed to his feet and sauntered over to her.

"Hey, honey."

"Stop it right now. You're not as charming as you think you are."

"I know that," Scott said with a grin that invited her to share his self-deprecating humor.

She tried to put herself in his shoes. If she'd had people of the opposite sex literally throwing themselves at her, she'd be the same way, right?

She shook her head and turned to walk away. But he stopped her with a hand on her wrist. His hand was big and strong, rough against her skin and totally at odds with his spoiled-rich-boy image.

"Wait. I think we got off on the wrong foot and I'd like to change that."

She still faced away, but glanced at him over her shoulder. There was something in his dark-brown gaze that held her captive and wouldn't let her walk away. Something that made her forget everything except him.

In an instant she realized she'd been using her disdain for the wealthy as a barrier against her attraction to him. Why did she have to pick today to let it drop?

She remembered what her father always said. *You can't con an honest man.* If Scott wasn't trying to manipulate her, then he wouldn't allow himself to be manipulated.

They only had three and a half more weeks of shooting. She should have made it that long. "Since we're on a break, let's get out of here and talk," he said.

"Talk?"

He arched an eyebrow at her. "Unless you had something else in mind."

She shook her head. Maybe before she'd heard him with Stevie, but not now. Honestly, not ever. Think of a con, she thought. Make it about that. But she didn't have a plan. She'd never been good at planning the actions even when she'd been a part of the game. She'd always been the honest one. Her father had said that with her eyes, no one ever expected a lie. "No. I…"

"Listen, I know there's something about me that rubs you the wrong way."

"It's not that." It wasn't fair that he'd be so perceptive when she couldn't get a handle on who he was. But it made an odd kind of sense. Only a man who knew what everyone else wanted would be able to effortlessly change into what they wanted.

"Then what? Because every other player on this tour has seen your smile except me."

"I didn't realize that," she said.

"Sure you did. You didn't care. Why is that, Raine?" he asked her. His voice dropped an octave.

She shivered at the sound of her name on his lips. She tried to remind herself that he was a trained actor, that this was all smoke and mirrors, but the finger rubbing her wrist made it feel like something more. And she remembered the other promise she'd made herself in high school other than getting the Oscar. No gamblers—ever.

* * *

Scott had spent the majority of his life on display, and he'd worked hard at projecting an image that said it didn't bother him. Truthfully, he hated it. Part of the reason he disappeared for months at a time was that he just couldn't stand to be social anymore. He got to the point where he couldn't tolerate anyone around him.

So why, then, was he standing here next to Raine Montgomery, who'd made it perfectly clear she didn't want to have anything to do with him? It wasn't the bet with Stevie. He'd wanted her since the moment he'd set eyes on her in Joel's office.

And she'd looked right through him. Maybe he was a closet masochist. Yeah, right. More likely, the lusty demon in his pants was making decisions for him again.

He wanted her. It didn't help that Vegas was his personal playground. The place that he came when he needed to blow off steam. And they were in the Chimera, the one hotel that he thought of as his home away from home.

The bet was nothing to him. An added bonus to something he'd already decided he wanted.

And there was nothing he liked more than a challenge. Especially one that came in a tempting package like Raine. She was petite but she packed a punch. Gaffers, lighting techs and stage hands all bent to her will.

Everyone joked that her God voice when she was in the booth was straight out of the Old Testament. She was firm and polite but unforgiving of mistakes. She was also lavish in her praise, and he'd seen how well respected she was.

He tucked his hand under her elbow and drew her away from the set through an open door that led to the casino floor. For the television show they were using a high-stakes poker room off the main casino.

"Where are you taking me?"

"To my lair," he said.

She laughed. "Okay, so you're not the big bad wolf."

"Who said that?"

"Stop trying to scare me. It won't work."

"I'm not trying to scare you. I'm attempting to find some common ground."

She pulled to a stop in a small alcove well out of the way of the foot traffic. "I'm not sure there is any."

"I know there is," he said, curving his body in front of hers to block them from the view of passersby.

She stared up at him, and he realized her eyes were a beautiful shade of deep blue. He'd never seen them up close before. Her eyes weren't what he'd expected. With her thick, dark, curly hair they should have been brown.

What else was she hiding?

"Why is this so important to you? I'm sorry I don't smile at you but I'll try to do it from now on."

Scott rubbed the back of his neck. "I want more than a smile."

"I don't date…" She lowered her head, staring at her feet. This woman was different from the director he'd seen on the set. Which was the real Raine?

"Actors? Gamblers? Rich men?" But he knew she meant him in particular. He'd bet half his fortune that she was like most women, who thought if they found some palatable word he wouldn't take it personally. But he knew from the way she watched him that it was Scott Rivers who made her nervous. Not his profession or his money.

"All of the above," she said, glancing up at him.

He stared into her eyes, losing himself there. He'd never admit it out loud but there was something in her eyes that called to his lonely soul. He wanted to explore that, find out exactly what it was. "I don't act anymore."

"That's right, you haven't since…when?" she asked.

"A lifetime ago." He remembered the day with a kind of fondness now. He'd been acting since he was nine months old. To say he'd chosen that profession was a huge exaggeration. He'd learned to act the same way he'd learned to walk and talk. Sometimes he wasn't sure that he knew how to really live.

"What about gambling? Can't deny that. You are being paid to play right now."

"Ah, but that's not really gambling, is it? I'm out there playing for charity and trying to outbluff the other contestants."

"And you always do it."

"Winning's important to me."

"Why?"

"Because losing sucks. Surely you've found that to be true."

"I have. That's why I play by the rules."

"What rules?"

"My rules for safe living. It's not that I'm not attracted to you. Who wouldn't be? But you're not worth the risk."

"Risk? Honey, you're safe with me."

"Don't call me honey. You call everyone that."

"Okay, but don't treat me like I'm nothing more than a list of professions or money. I want a chance to get to know the real Raine."

She shook her head. "I don't have time. And we both signed a waiver saying no fraternization with the cast or crew."

"Live a little, Raine. Take a chance. We both have some free time."

She bit her lower lip, and he realized that he was pushing her. He analyzed Raine and the situation. If he backed down now, she'd never let him get her alone again. But maybe… "I dare you."

"What?"

"I dare you to go out with me. I dare you to see past the flashbulbs and the gossip-sheet rumors about me."

Two

Damn him. That was all she could think as she stood there contemplating the dare.

She wanted to accept it. Not only to get back at him—because it would give her a chance to put her half-formed idea of making him fall for her into action—but also because she liked him. She was attracted to him.

But she wasn't sure what was motivating Scott. Was it just the money he'd wagered with the rocker or did he want more? And was she really willing to risk her job just so she could one-up him? And she definitely was going to one-up this man. Did she really want to take a chance on another man hurting her?

A dare.

Still, it was hard to change her habits. She was a risk taker by nature, and every instinct in her wanted to take him up on his dare. To prove to him he wasn't the hot stuff he thought he was.

A dare.

She'd spent a lifetime tamping down the urges of her wild blood. That was what Grandma Nan had always called it when Raine got into scrapes at school. And in her younger days she'd gotten into more than a few of them.

She'd never been able to resist a dare.

How had this man known? What was it about his dark-brown eyes that enabled him to see past the protective layers others never noticed were there?

In truth she knew it wasn't arrogance. The man had a swarm of adoring people following him around day and night. She wondered how long they'd be alone in the alcove before one of his fans found him.

"What's the matter? Scared you can't handle me off the set where you're not in charge?" he asked in that silky tone of his.

She realized he was so used to getting his way that it never occurred to him she'd turn him down. And it irked her that she was thinking about accepting his invitation. But she was definitely going to make him work for it.

"I think we covered this already," she replied. "I'm not scared of any man."

"Then I'll pick you up in your suite at eight. Dressy casual. Be prepared for the night of your life."

She wrapped her arms around her waist. His words, the delivery and tone, were exactly like her father's. Every birthday he'd called her, promising her the moon, and for eight long years she'd believed him.

"You know nothing about me, Scott. How can you guarantee me the night of my life?" she asked carefully. Maybe going wasn't a good idea, no matter how tempting he was. Actually, because of how tempting he was. She'd forgotten her own rules. No matter what spin he put on it, Scott Rivers was a gambler. He gambled every day on life, taking risks and issuing dares.

"Touché. That was arrogant." He grinned at her.

"Just a tad."

"I'd like to say it won't happen again, but…"

This time she laughed at him. He was very charming, and she didn't care if it was practiced. This was the man she had to be careful around. The one she'd find it so easy to fall for. For just this once, though, she wanted to enjoy basking in his laughter.

"How about a night of getting to know each other?" he asked, propping one hand on the wall behind her and angling his body closer to hers.

The heat of his body swamped her. She struggled to keep her pulse steady, but it had picked up the minute he'd put his hand on the wall next to her head. He captured one of her curls with his fingers and toyed with the strand. "Why is this important to you?" she asked.

He ran his finger down the side of her face, his touch tentative and very gentle. For the first time in her life she felt…special. Not the go-to girl or the can-handle-anything woman. But as if she was actually the one who needed to be treasured and pampered by a man. *He's just playing you,* she reminded herself. But she liked the way he was treating her—which unsettled what she thought she knew about herself.

He leaned even closer to her. She inhaled his spicy aftershave and the smell of his breath mints. Her breath probably smelled like garlic from the scampi she'd had for lunch. This was why she didn't do the fairy tale thing.

"I can't get you out of my head," he said.

She stopped thinking about her breath and stared up at this man who had to be putting her on. "Lust, eh? I'm not really cover-model material."

"No, you're not. You have something so unique. Something that's just Raine."

His words touched her and she had to swallow. She told herself he was a consummate actor, even though it had been a while since he'd tried his hand at that. A part of her wanted to believe him, but another part was afraid. She'd grown up with her father, the accomplished con man who could promise anything and make everyone including Raine believe it.

"Don't say things like that to me. I prefer honesty."

"As you pointed out, we don't know each other. I just want a chance."

"One chance. But no more of those mushy romance lines that you've doled out to a hundred other women."

"Jeez, I'm not sure you'll fit in my car with that chip on your shoulder. And I think we both know I haven't had a hundred women."

"I don't care if you've had a thousand."

"You will," he said. Lowering his head, he kissed her. His lips brushed hers, and when she opened her mouth to breathe, his tongue slipped past her lips and into her mouth. He tasted her with long, languid strokes of his tongue. She tipped her head to grant him greater access.

Still he didn't hurry. He just leaned there next to her, taking his time and exploring the fire that she'd never wanted to acknowledge was between them. Awareness spread down her body, and she relished the taste of him.

The world fell away and she swayed when his hands skimmed down her back and over her hips and he tugged her closer to him. The wall was solid behind her, and he was solid heat pressed to the front of her. She felt trapped and oddly free because the decision was taken out of her hands. This was the most daring thing she'd done in years.

Her pulse raced, and she knew that something she'd caged long ago had broken free. She reached for his shoulders, but he pulled back.

"Eight," he said, and turned on his heel and walked away.

Scott went back to the set, but he was off his game for the rest of the day. He knew no one else observed it but he felt it inside. For the first time in fifteen years he was distracted by someone. He wasn't just focused on his own pleasures. It was an odd feeling and he wasn't sure he liked it.

But the only time he felt alive was when he was doing something risky, which was why he'd made the bet and was pursuing Raine. Who would've thought pursuing a petite brunette would be the challenge he'd been searching for?

Scott almost blew a really big hand, but brought his attention back to the game at the last minute.

They wrapped for the day, and he noticed that Raine stayed far away from him. Even when she came out of her booth, she gave him and the other players a wide berth. Scott finished up the conversation he was having with Stevie and started slowly stalking her.

She glared at him once so he knew she was aware of his presence. He laughed. She was so sassy and spunky that he couldn't help himself. She might prefer safety and routine, but nothing could dampen the innate fire that burned inside her.

Why was she even trying to hide it? He knew then that the secrets he wanted to unlock in Raine were somehow tied to that passion.

She moved toward the exit, and Scott deftly followed her, blocking the one door off the set. He folded his arms over his chest and leaned back against the wall. She tossed her hair and pivoted on her heel, facing away from him.

"You still have that magic touch with the ladies," a droll voice said behind him.

Scott turned to see one of his closest friends, Hayden MacKenzie—the newly married Hayden. "What can I say? I should bottle my charm."

"Well, it is legendary. Does she not know that? Want me to go talk to her?"

"What are we—in junior high?"

"I don't know. I didn't go to junior high," Hayden said.

Hayden had attended an exclusive boys' school back east. Scott had met him in Europe when they'd both had too much money, too much anger and too much time on their hands. The other man stood a few inches taller than Scott.

"So how's wedded life? Still bliss?"

Hayden smiled and for the first time since Scott had met him he saw a kind of peace in Hayden's eyes. "Can't complain. In fact, Shelby and I are having a dinner party on Friday. Can you come?"

"I might have plans."

"You can bring her with you. Max is flying down from Vancouver, where he's brokering a deal. Deacon and Kylie will be there."

"Okay. But it'll be just me. I don't want Max to feel like the Lone Ranger."

"You know Max. He's never alone for long. See you at nine on Friday."

Hayden walked away and Scott watched his friend leave. He wasn't sure he wanted to be surrounded by his bachelor buddies who'd given up the single life. Scott had been alone for so long.

"Is everything okay?"

He glanced down at Raine. "Yes. Why?"

"Hayden owns the Chimera. I wasn't sure if there was a problem."

"Hayden and I go way back. Besides, he'd speak to you if there was a problem, wouldn't he?"

She shrugged. "I guess. Listen, I'm going to have to work late, editing today's shoot. So we'll have to cancel dinner."

He'd never had to work so hard with a woman, and a part of him toyed with the idea of just stopping his pursuit. He could afford to lose the bet to Stevie. But there was something about Raine that wouldn't let him do that.

"No problem. We'll go whenever you can. My plans are fluid," he said, watching her carefully.

She put her hands on her hips and stared up at him. "I'm not sure how to say this…."

"Stop trying to find excuses. I'm not going to ask you to strip naked in front of a crowd of people. It's just dinner."

She dropped her arms and glanced around the set, which had cleared out except for one camera guy, who was still putting his gear away. "I'm not usually like this. You seem to bring it out in me. Are you sure you want to have dinner?"

"Yes. I'm not feeding you a bunch of BS, Raine. Believe me, I wouldn't work this hard for a woman if I wasn't really interested."

There was a hint of vulnerability on her face before she carefully concealed it. "I'm free now. How about something casual?"

"It's a little early for dinner."

"Maybe we could go do something."

"What do you have in mind?" he asked, sensing with Raine it was better to let her take the lead at first. He sensed she was used to being in charge on the job and off as well.

"Minigolf?"

No way. He had a reputation to live up to. "What are we…ready for the retirement home?"

"Well, what do *you* have in mind?" she asked in that quick-tempered way of hers.

"How much time do you have?" he asked, struggling not to smile at her show of temper.

She consulted her watch. "Four hours."

"One round at the roulette table. Winner picks the next activity."

"I don't gamble."

"Why not?"

"I just don't."

"Rumor has it that you were once a big-time player."

"The *National Enquirer* intimated you had sex with an alien on your yacht in the Mediterranean."

"Then you were a big-time player," he said.

She threw her head back and laughed. "Okay, you win. I'll play roulette with you, but only one game. Whoever wins picks the activity."

"I don't lose," he said, warning her.

"Neither do I."

Raine rubbed her sweaty palms against her jeans and stood in front of the roulette table. She was intimately familiar with this game, having grown up a few blocks from the casinos in Atlantic City. She'd spent her child-hood on the boardwalk, staring in at her father, who'd spend a few days playing roulette when he couldn't scrape together enough money to stake himself to a poker game.

Just one small bet. That was all she had to do. She wasn't going to become addicted to gambling by plac-ing one bet. She'd bet Scott on this one game and then she'd take him to the Keno diner on the second floor, sit with him in a vinyl booth and bore him to death so he would move on.

Conning him didn't seem like such an easy thing to do just now. She felt as if she was being torn in two, and the balance and serenity she'd worked so hard to find in her life were now gone.

Her heart was beating too fast, and every minute she spent in his presence made her like him more.

"What are you waiting for?" he asked, making her realize that she'd been staring at the rows of black and red spaces for too long.

She scrambled for an answer. She was used to thinking on her feet in the high-pressure world of tele-vision. "You have to have a strategy."

"For roulette?" he asked. "Be careful, Raine. This is just chance. Odds or evens, black or red. That's all you have to decide."

"Well, we all aren't you, Mr. Lucky. I need a strategy. Give me a minute."

Turning away from him, she closed her eyes. Com-ing to Vegas had been a struggle. She wasn't a gambler by profession, but her heart was always ready to bet on something.

Every day she walked past the odds board in the lobby and mentally bet on something, anything. Prize fights, European sporting events, even the outcome of certain reality shows. She was contractually forbidden from betting on their show, but in her mind she bet every time.

She'd watched her father and brother both spiral out of control and into addiction. Right now they were both living hand-to-mouth existences. And she couldn't help them. When she sent money, they only gambled it away, and when she visited, they wanted her to run one more con. A big score so they'd be set for life.

She was being silly. One little roulette bet wasn't going to turn her into an addict. She took a deep breath and looked up at Scott. "Okay, I'm ready."

"What's your lucky number?" he asked.

She didn't have a lucky number, didn't believe that luck came from numbers or rabbits' feet.

"Don't have one?" he asked, putting his arm around her waist and leaning closer.

They were in the main casino, where anyone could see them. She inched away from him. "No. Why should I?"

"No reason. Mine is thirteen. Want to use it this time?"

"No. I'll take fourteen."

"Okay," he said, reaching around her to drop a few casino chips on the table.

"What are you doing?" she asked. What did it say about the man that he had a pocketful of casino chips?

"This is on me."

She shrugged and placed her bet. She put her chip only on the number, not bettering her odds by playing the color.

"You're going for the bigger payoff just like a real gambler would," he said.

He had no idea. She'd watched her father at the roulette table for so long that she'd played the way he would. His words didn't reassure her, and it took all of her courage to stand her ground and not turn and run from the casino. Her hand actually trembled as she saw the croupier begin the play.

Scott captured her hand and rubbed it against his T-shirt-clad chest. "Don't sweat it, honey. This is just for fun."

She looked up at him and felt the waves of reassurance in him. Despite his playboy image and the way he seemed to glide through life unaffected, she sensed a rock-solid part of this man.

"I know."

"When I win, I'm going to take you for a ride on my Harley out into the desert with the warm wind blowing all around us. Then we'll have dinner at my favorite hole-in-the-wall Mexican place."

That didn't sound dangerous. It sounded fun, thrilling. She'd never been on a motorcycle and a part of her had always wanted to ride one. Especially if she was pressed up against Scott's back. She'd have an excuse

to touch him and not have to worry about the consequences for once in her life, not taking the same safe
route she'd always chosen.

But he had dared her—and she couldn't pass it up.
"I don't know what I'll do when I win. Probably something safe and boring."

He smiled at her then. His expression was so tender
that the sounds of the casino faded away, and there was
only the two of them. "Nothing with you could be
boring."

She turned away from the intensity in his eyes and
focused on the table. The ball jumped and bounced
and finally landed on fourteen. Raine couldn't believe
it.

"I won."

"I saw," he said. His arms came around her waist and
he held her to him. "Maybe my luck is rubbing off on
you."

"I didn't realize that luck felt like a muscled, masculine body."

He dropped a fierce kiss on her lips. "Luck comes
in all kinds of packages."

She had the feeling he was talking about more than
slot machines and Vegas winnings. "Bad luck sure
does."

"Hey, no talk of bad luck," he said.

"I can't believe this. You lost," she said. And she
won. After years of carefully avoiding taking any kind
of risk, the first time she bet someone, she won.

"I know."

She stepped away from him, fighting the urge to dance around. She won. For the first time she could understand the appeal of gambling. But she realized her euphoria had as much to do with the fact that she was with Scott as it did with winning.

"Does this ever happen to you?" she asked.

"About as often as I make it with my alien lover."

She laughed and felt free in a way she hadn't in a long time. Scott reminded her of what life could be when she let go of the tight control she kept on herself.

"What now?"

He picked up her winnings. "Let's go cash out, and then the rest of the night is up to you."

The glow of victory still hung around Raine as they stepped away from the cashier and she pocketed her winnings.

"So what's the plan? I think we've got a few hours until you have to be in the editing room."

She glanced at her watch, then tipped her head to the side, studying him. "How do you feel about going to Red Rock? They have a nature trail that's supposed to be pretty awesome and it's not that far from here. I haven't had time to check it out yet."

"Sounds good. I'll drive, unless you want to?"

"No, you can drive. I'm sharing the production van with Tim and Leslie."

Just then Scott became aware of a group of three women who were eyeing him. He knew the second they recognized him. They took a few steps toward him, but Scott wrapped his arm around Raine and made for the exit. She shoved her elbow against his stomach but he refused to budge. He suspected she was worried about Joel or someone from the show catching them together, but he liked the way she felt tucked up against him. "You have a choice."

"Of what?" she asked as they left the casino behind and walked out into the warm spring afternoon.

He put on his sunglasses and led her toward the employee parking garage. Hayden kept the top floor of the garage for his own private vehicles and allowed Scott to store his there, as well. Sometimes Scott thought his entire life was just one long travelogue as he moved from one location to another.

"Of how you want to go," he said, leading her to the garage elevator. He pressed the button for the top floor and then inserted his security key to access the parking level.

"I keep a Hummer H2, a Porsche Boxster and a Harley-Davidson Screamin' Eagle V-Rod here. I don't think we can off-road at Red Rock so the Porsche or the bike would be a better choice."

"Your cars cost more than my house does back in Glendale, California."

He shrugged. "It's just money."

She put one hand on her hip and narrowed her eyes. "Not to everyone."

"Is this going to be an issue?"

She said nothing, and he knew it was. He'd dated women with Raine's outlook before. Some women honestly had a problem with the insane amount of money he had. He recognized it could be an issue and he hated that because the money was part of who he was.

"I started working when I was nine months old," he explained.

She dropped her hand. "I know."

"Then you can't expect me to be poor. I spent my entire childhood earning that money."

"Should I grovel for forgiveness?"

Realizing he had his own problems with this issue, he forced himself to relax. "Maybe later."

"I have money issues in general. It was just a shock to hear you rattle off your list of vehicles."

"Can you get over it?" he asked teasingly.

She tipped her head to the side and gave him one of those looks of hers that cut past all the images he'd cultivated over the years and burned straight to the bone. He should probably stay here in Vegas where he fit in. Out in nature he always felt more like the fraud he was. No longer the actor on a set but out in the elements.

"Yeah," she finally said. "I can get over it—especially if you let me drive the Porsche."

"Didn't you hit the security rail with the production van yesterday?"

She wrinkled her brow. "That story was grossly exaggerated. No damage was done to the van."

"I'll think about letting you drive my car on the way back."

He crossed the parking lot to the Porsche convertible. Opening the trunk, he pulled out two baseball caps. "If we're taking this car you'll need a hat. The sun is hot with the top down. You want the Yankees or the Red Sox?"

"We can't ride in the same car wearing those hats."

"Sure we can. You like to fight. This will make people believe we have a reason."

"I don't like to argue. You're the one who's contrary."

"Really? I'll keep that in mind."

"Why do you have East Coast hats? I thought you grew up in L.A."

"I did. The Sox cap is Hayden's. I picked the Yankees just to needle him."

He opened her door for her. She gave him a strange look before sliding into the car.

"What was that look?"

"Most guys don't hold the door."

"Most guys don't have my mom. She's a stickler for manners and men holding doors."

"She sounds like my kind of woman."

"She's…fierce, I guess. She made sure no one took advantage of me when I was a kid. She still watches out for me now."

"What about your dad?"

"He backs her up when she needs him. But he's content to let her lead the way."

"Sounds like they have a good marriage."

"They do. What about your folks?" he asked as he put down the top on the convertible. Once it was down, he backed out of the parking space and headed to the exit.

"My folks are divorced. My mom remarried when I was sixteen. We're not real close."

"What about your dad?"

"He lives on the East Coast so I don't see him."

"My folks live in Malibu. I see them all the time when I'm in Los Angeles."

She said nothing as he maneuvered the car onto 215 and headed toward Red Rock. "Too bad I didn't think of asking you out sooner. We could have applied for a rock climbing permit."

"I think I'd have a heart attack if I tried to do that."

"It's easy."

"Sure it is. Easy to fall."

"What kind of guy do you think I am? I'd never let you fall."

"Stop it. You sound too good to be true. Remember, I'm on to you and your smooth-talking ways."

If only she were right and he were feeding her lines. But there was something too real about Raine. He'd felt her pain when she'd spoken quietly of her lack of parental contact. He wanted to sweep her into his arms and promise she'd never be alone again.

No matter how much she intrigued him, this would be the same as every other relationship in his life. Fleeting and memorable.

Three

A tense silence filled the car as they entered the Red Rock Canyon National Conservation Area. The area had some of the best examples of the Mojave Desert terrain in Nevada. Raine had never been an outdoorsy girl. But there was something so clean about being here now. Especially compared to the overdeveloped Vegas strip where she'd been spending all her time. She closed her eyes and breathed deeply.

"You okay?"

"Yeah," she said, realizing that she was. The bet with Scott, the constant fear she felt being close to gambling, even her own tension about his interest in her dropped away. Within moments there was nothing but the two of them and nature.

"Sure?"

"Yes, I was just thinking how different this is from Vegas. I have to warn you that even though I suggested this, I'm not really a nature girl."

"That's okay. I am."

"You're a nature girl?"

"Ha, nature boy. Seriously, I spend all my free time outside."

For a man who had the world at his fingertips, he spent a lot of his time like any other guy his age.

"I still can't believe this place is so close to our hotel," she said, offering a tentative olive branch to Scott. This was a mistake, she thought. Her gut had said it from the beginning, but she'd foolishly thought she could dip one foot into the world she'd always forbidden herself.

She'd been out of the game too long to pull a con on this guy and she knew it. Besides, her hormones were making it difficult to concentrate on conning him. She wanted to just tip her head back and enjoy being around Scott. This man who'd been acting before he could walk or talk. This man who made his living betting on everything under the sun.

"Me, neither," he said. He pulled into the visitor center parking lot. Turning to look at her, he tugged off his sunglasses, but his eyes still weren't visible under the brim of his Red Sox cap. "Have you been here before?"

His tone was conversational. No more flirting. She wasn't disappointed. Really, she wasn't. "No. I read about it in the area information in my room."

"I've been here a few times. How adventurous are you feeling?" he asked, a hint of speculation in his eyes.

"Moderate." She suspected he was talking about more than the trail. And she'd never been adventurous; she'd always chosen the safe and sane route. Even her career, which was in a field that was constantly changing, had always been stable. Being unadventurous was her one goal in life.

"What would it take to bump that up?" he asked.

"I don't know. Maybe getting to know you a little better?"

He nodded and put his sunglasses back on. "What kind of shoes are you wearing?"

"Why?" she asked.

"There's a trail that involves some climbing and leads to a waterfall. But if you don't have hiking boots on…"

"I don't. Plus I'm not really very athletic."

"Then how about an easy trail?" He pulled a well-thumbed-through guidebook from the side pocket on the door. "Can you do two miles round trip?"

"I guess driving through the park is out of the question?"

Considering he'd only arrived in Vegas a few days ago, Raine thought, he seemed very comfortable and at home here. But then he was a gambler, so he'd probably spent a fair amount of time in Sin City. She had the feeling that he was always at home, wherever he was.

She envied him that. She was still searching to find that kind of peace deep inside herself. And she knew she needed things around her. The same things, the same routines, the same people, to find her comfort level.

He was a chameleon, she reminded herself. He changed to fit all of his surroundings, and she'd do well to remember that.

"Hell, yes, it's out of the question. I really want to do the Ice Box trail but I don't think you're up to it."

"Fine. I can go two miles. I do more than that at the Galleria during the holidays."

Raine went into the ranger station to register them while Scott gathered supplies. She met him back in the parking lot five minutes later and found him talking baseball with two guys.

"There's my lady," he said, leaving the men and joining her.

"I'm your lady?" she asked.

She'd never belonged to any man before. She'd had sex with exactly two men in her life. Her first boyfriend had been in college, and that had lasted one semester. The second guy had been looking for a job in the industry and saw her as the most expedient route to where he wanted to go.

She knew that she was to blame for her love life. She didn't trust men or even want to trust them. She liked her career and got by focusing on that. This current situation with Scott was just a con. She tried to remember that, but it was hard.

"I want you to be my lady," he said, leading the way out of the parking lot and toward the Moenkopi Loop.

She wished he'd stop saying things like that. But it fit perfectly with his bet, and she realized she had to keep her mind sharp. That was another of her dad's lessons—don't forget the end goal.

But Scott was different. He made her want to reevaluate her life. Take stock in where she was—almost thirty and still single. And he made her want to change things, to forget she was very happy with who she was.

"Why are you here?" she asked when they found the trail and walked side by side. Get to know the mark, she thought.

"You asked me to come."

"Ha-ha, smart-ass. I meant, why are you doing the show?" she asked, focusing on Scott and not on how easily the rules of grifting were returning to her.

"I'm friends with Joel Tanner. He needed a name to take to the networks."

Joel was the executive producer on the show. He was riding a string of popular hits on television that threatened to rival Aaron Spelling's golden touch in the eighties and nineties. Raine found him to be a fair man most of the time. She didn't have to deal with him too often, which she liked. He was also her boss, so if this thing with Scott didn't work out, Scott had the inside track on making sure she never worked again. "That was nice of you."

"That's the kind of guy I am," he said, arching his eyebrow at her.

"I think you adjust to being the right guy for every situation." She'd observed it from watching him on the set. Scott was literally the right man in every situation. Just like with those guys in the parking lot, he could fit in with any group at a moment's notice. It was a little unnerving to Raine because she'd never really fit in anywhere.

He stopped walking. The sun was dipping into the horizon, and a nice breeze stirred through the under-brush. "What's that mean?"

She heard something moving through the shrubs and edged closer to Scott. He made her feel safe. For a minute she forgot that she didn't need anyone to protect her and just basked in the warmth of his body.

"Well?"

She should have kept her mouth shut. "That you fit in everywhere. I've seen you with poker players, laid-back and joking. With Joel, serious and discussing busi-ness. With those baseball fans, just another guy upset by the steroids scandal."

"I'm well-rounded."

She heard that noise again. "Did you hear that? What kind of animals are out here?"

"Don't worry about them."

"I'm not."

He gave her a skeptical look. "Are you worried about me?"

"I'm not scared of you," she said, forcing her gaze away from the small brush and up to the panoramic view. Nature was nice and everything, but suddenly she just wanted to be back in Vegas where she was dealing with things she could see and understand. Whatever was moving in the brush…that was unknown.

"I'm still waiting to hear what you meant by your comment."

The key to a good con was to act like you believed the situation was real up to the moment you walked away, she remembered. And it wasn't hard to do with Scott because she liked him. Deep inside, a part of her mourned the relationship they could have had.

"I don't know. It seems like you change in each situation. You become exactly what the setting demands. Almost like you're acting."

"Maybe I am," he said. "But that's the only way I know how to be."

Scott eased the car to the side of the road just outside the Red Rocks Park. He'd steered the conversation away from himself after she'd dropped her bomb about acting being his only way of coping. And he'd kept them moving on the path. What would she say if she knew he was doing this for a bet?

What the hell had he been thinking? Stevie really pissed him off, because now Scott knew that he had to overcome those obstacles in addition to the natural weariness that Raine exhibited around him.

He never accurately counted the cost when he took a bet like this one. It didn't matter that he'd dared himself to spend time with Raine long before Stevie had caught him getting the cold shoulder and made it into a wager. The results were the same. He felt wild and out of control. He liked it too much to complain about it.

But that didn't mean he wanted her to see his flaws. He'd carefully cultivated a hip image to make it seem as if he was flawless. He wasn't one of those child stars who'd gone down the road to addiction, because his parents simply wouldn't have tolerated it. And Scott was in his heart of hearts a good guy.

Raine deserved to know that guy. Not the man who'd made a bet about getting her into bed. A stronger man might be able to walk away from Raine. But Scott couldn't. There was something about her that had already gotten under his skin, keeping him in a state of semiarousal all the time.

He shut off the engine as he stopped on the shoulder. Time to let Raine live a little. She was too buttoned up most of the time, and he suspected she was hiding.

"What are we stopping for? Is something wrong with the car?" she asked. She'd had her head back against the headrest but sat up, uncrossing her long legs and pushing her baseball cap off her head.

Her hair was unruly and he liked the way it looked. Her face was flushed from the exercise. He wanted nothing more than to just lean over and bury his face against her neck. Inhale the fragrance of woman and kiss her there.

This was doing nothing to cool him off. But he suspected nothing was going to do that. Raine was a fire in his blood.

"No. I thought I'd let you drive," he said. He wanted more than one afternoon with her. The intriguing Ms. Raine Montgomery was still a mystery to be solved.

"Really?" she asked, her eyes widening.

He leaned back in the seat, crossing his arms over his chest. "Unless you don't want to."

"Of course I want to," she said.

"Do you have any tickets on your license?" he asked, to tease her.

She shook her head, very earnest now, and he ached inside at how innocent she looked.

"Are you kidding? The words *safe driver* were invented for me."

He realized that the bet was going to haunt him, because a woman like Raine was too soft to ever forgive that action. In fact, he wasn't too sure he could forgive himself.

He forced himself to continue the game he'd started. "Hmm. Let me get this straight. You don't have adventures, no tickets, no dating. What do you call that incident with the guardrail?"

She grabbed his hands in hers. "A fluke. Really I'm so safe I usually drive *under* the speed limit."

"What do you do for fun?" he asked because he really wanted to know. Whatever she did, he'd take it up. Even if she said minigolf.

"I have a life," she said defensively.

He'd been teasing her and hadn't expected this reaction. "I was kidding. And hoping you didn't say minigolf."

"I know, but when you say it like that...I seem like

a really boring person who does nothing but work. And there's nothing wrong with minigolf."

In her voice he heard the criticism she must endure from time to time. Like the comments he got about his lack of direction and seemingly unfocused lifestyle. Few people realized the extent of the charitable work he did or that he'd spent the past five years bailing out friends who'd lost it all in the dot-com bust.

"You could be a lady with an exciting job," he said, because he knew she liked her life. Raine wasn't a woman to stay in a job she didn't love.

He slid his hand along the back of her seat, capturing a handful of her curls in his hand. She had the softest damned hair he'd ever touched.

"I think I am. You know, I've wanted to be in show business since I was in junior high school."

He wanted to know every detail of her childhood. Maybe it would help him figure out what made her tick. He already knew she wasn't close to her parents. "Really? Did you always want to stay behind the camera?"

She tilted her head back, rubbing her scalp against his wrist. He changed his grip on her hair so that he could rub her head.

"Yes. I'm not really a spotlight person. And I really like telling everyone what to do."

"I've never noticed that."

"I must be being too easy on you." She turned to face him and gave him a long, measuring look.

"Actually, I'd say the opposite is true. Everyone else gets teased but me. Even Stevie, with his skull-and-crossbones tattoo, gets the soft edge of your tongue, but I see only the…"

"Say it," she said.

"The defensive side of you. What is it about me?" he asked.

"Nothing. Don't project your feelings onto me."

"I'm not. It can't be that I'm a quasi-celebrity."

She snorted. "You're an über-celebrity. But that has nothing to do with my supposed attitude."

"It's not the money thing, either, though we've already established that doesn't earn me any favors."

"I don't know what you're driving at."

"Me, neither, but I'm a patient man, honey. And I'm not going to be satisfied until I figure you out."

"I thought you were going to let me drive."

"I am."

She calmly unfastened her seat belt and opened the door. "Are you sure?"

He climbed out of the car and met her halfway around it. "Stop asking me or I'll change my mind."

She tipped her head to one side. It was something he knew she did when she was pondering something. He'd seen her do it on the set a few times, and earlier before she'd chosen number fourteen on the roulette table. "No, you won't. You don't say things you don't mean."

"How do you know that?" he asked, because he thought he played that one close to the chest. He liked to be the rambling man. The one with no commitments, the one no one asked anything of.

"I've been watching you while we shoot," she said.

That was why he'd accepted Stevie's bet. It gave him an added incentive to stay on this rocky road that led to Raine. He'd realized after the first day on the set that he was interested in her, but it had taken him a little longer to ascertain that she wanted him, too. "Really? And you picked that up."

"Yes. You're a very rock-solid man."

He couldn't help but grin. "Around you, anyway."

"Was that a sex crack?"

"Yes, ma'am, it was. I don't want you to put me into some buddy box. I'm not doing this to be your buddy."

"You're doing this to get me into bed?"

Yes, but he was smart enough not to admit it. "Nah, but I figure letting you drive the Porsche will make it more likely that you'll let me kiss you when we get back to the hotel."

"We've already kissed," she said.

"So?"

"You want more?"

"Don't you?"

"I haven't decided yet. You're a little too…dangerous."

"I'm harmless," he said, and he was for her. He'd never met another woman he wanted as badly as he wanted Raine.

"Tell that to my heart," she said quietly, slipping behind the wheel.

Raine got out of the car at the front of the Chimera, tossing the keys to Scott. She was starting to feel like a manic-depressive. Scott evoked so many different re-actions in her. She felt the same sense of panic she always did.

She glanced at her watch and thought she still had forty-five minutes before she had to meet Larry at the editing suite. But she needed a break. A chance to quiet herself and figure out what was really going on here.

"We cut it kind of close. I'd better run."

"Wait up," he said.

"I can't."

She pivoted on her heel and started toward the hotel and then realized that she was running away. She'd promised herself when she left Atlantic City more than ten years ago that her running days were behind her.

She turned back around. Scott was standing by his car watching her. What was she going to say? She knew she had to keep it light. She could do that. Just flirt a little and he'd never guess at the turmoil inside her.

"Let me give the keys to the valet and I'll walk you back to the editing suite."

She nodded and slipped away from the crowd to wait for him near the front doors. She hated this about herself. This thing she'd never been able to control. As a child she remembered countless days standing on the boardwalk while her father played grueling, hours-long poker games and her mother was working two jobs. She looked like an abandoned waif so her father could take money from well-meaning people who took pity on her.

Scott made her feel that way again. Unsure of

herself. She shook her head and pushed away from the wall. This wasn't his fault, but hers. He reminded her of all the tantalizing and forbidden things she liked. And that made her uneasy.

She knew she was losing control of her own con. Especially when she realized two P.A.s—production assistants—were standing on the valet line. Damn. She had to get away now.

"You okay?" he asked.

She pulled the baseball cap lower on her head and walked at a clipped pace toward the hotel door. "I think I see a couple of P.A.s from the show."

"I'm an expert at evasion," he said, pulling her under his shoulder and hustling them through the lobby and into an alcove. He kept her tucked up against his side, blocking her with his body.

"How's that?" he asked.

"Good." Too good, she thought. He was an expert at evasion. Not only of the kind they just did but of the emotional kind. Every time she got close to figuring him out, he danced out of her reach again.

She pushed against his chest, but he wouldn't budge.

"What are you doing?" he asked.

"Trying to get away from you." She bit her lip as soon as the words left her mouth. Great. She wasn't supposed to show him any weakness.

"Why?"

"I'm not used to that kind of exercise. I think you wore me out," she lied, but then made the mistake of glancing up at him. His face was classically handsome, with a strong jaw and firm lips…lips she wanted to feel against her own.

She leaned up and toward him, then realized what she was doing and pulled back. Get a grip, she told herself. You can't kiss him until you have some objectivity back in place. Still, she wanted to.

To hell with her plans. She wanted to feel his mouth moving on hers and his arms around her. Really around her, not just holding her to keep her concealed from prying eyes.

"Thanks for letting me drive your car," she said, praying he'd accept the subject change.

"No problem. Next time I'll get us some bikes so we can do some of the awesome bike trails up there."

She shuddered. She'd suggested Red Rock because it would get them away from the rest of the cast and crew who might see them. But she wasn't sure she could go back and try anything else. "Are you kidding? I can barely make it around the block at my house in Glendale. I'm never going to be able to bike down a trail."

"Well, something else then. Maybe I'll let you take the Harley for a spin sometime, too."

"I don't think so," she said. "I think the coast is clear now."

He glanced over his shoulder and nodded, stepping away. She following him through the air-conditioned luxury of the Chimera's lobby.

He put his hand under her elbow as they walked. She knew it was an old-fashioned gesture, but she liked it.

She also liked the way he slowed his pace to hers. Hell, she plain liked too much about Scott Rivers.

And that was her main problem. She didn't want to like him. Not his friendly smile or his sexy tush. She wanted to not notice those things and find a way back to the adversarial relationship they'd had before this afternoon.

When they reached the bank of elevators, they waited with a small crowd. Raine felt unkempt in her jeans and T-shirt, sweaty from being outdoors, and out of place in the world of the well-groomed people.

Scott slid his arm around her waist and tugged her under his shoulder, holding her protectively.

"What are you doing?" she asked, hoping that he didn't hear the trembling note in her voice. This wasn't like her. But she'd always wanted to be held like this.

"Using you."

Now that was something she was used to from the men in her life. Her backbone stiffened as she realized that her con was the only safe way she could stay around Scott. Otherwise she'd give him too much ammunition to hurt her. "As what?"

"Camouflage. I think those women over there are hunting men."

He gestured toward three women with well-coiffed hair, dressed like Paris Hilton, in haute couture from their scantily covered midriffs to their Jimmy Choo clad feet.

No one could ever mistake Raine as part of that group. She glanced down at her scruffy old Nikes and jeans. "And you're the next target on the list?"

He arched his eyebrows at her. "At the risk of sounding arrogant…yes."

She put her arm around his back and hugged him close to her. Those girls reminded her of Missy Talbot. Immediately she felt as if she was in high school again. Only this time, she was on the arm of the sexiest man in the room.

It was a heady feeling for about a second, before she remembered why he was here. This was his game—but she was playing it to win. She put her arm around his lean waist. "How's this?"

"Slip your hand into my front pocket."

She narrowed her eyes at him. She was physically tired from hiking, emotionally fatigued from the conflict inside her about Scott, and she wanted him too much to keep her hands to herself. "Why?"

"For effect. So they'll know I'm yours and to keep their hands off."

She pushed her hand into his front pants pocket, brushing past the casino chips and feeling the heat of his thigh through the lining.

"Now move it down a little and over."

She snatched her hand back. "Pervert."

He laughed. That deep rumbling one he had that made her want to just bask in it all day. This was why she needed to get away. She was forgetting the lessons she'd learned early in life. A con man wasn't a bad or evil man; grifters were gregarious people with larger-than-life personalities. That was how they lured in their victims.

"What are you thinking?" he asked, suddenly very serious.

"Nothing." Scott was a nice guy on one level and she thought about what she'd do if this was real and not some bet he was trying to win. He wouldn't deserve the baggage she was packing. "I'm thinking that I know better than to get involved with a sex fiend."

"I'm not a fiend. I just like things…earthy."

"You're dangerous to womankind. I can't believe I helped you out. You would have been fine on your own."

The elevator doors opened and he led her into the car, taking a spot against the back wall. No one entered behind them, and once the doors closed they were alone.

She busied herself pressing the button for her floor. She hoped to get a shower before she had to work all night. Glancing over at Scott, she realized he was watching her.

"What? Do I have dirt on my face?" she asked, rubbing her cheeks.

He said nothing, just closed the small gap between them. He took her face in his hands and tilted her head back. "You look wonderful. Too wonderful for a man like me."

"What does that mean?" she asked, afraid she knew the answer. He was, after all, a man who'd made a bet he could get her into bed.

Instead of answering her, he lowered his head and brushed his lips against hers. Her lips fluttered open under his, and his tongue slowly penetrated the barrier of her mouth. She was aware that she was allowing him to use sex to change the subject…but she didn't want to stop him now.

Four

Raine tasted like the wild wind right before a summer storm. He tunneled his fingers into her hair and tilted her head back to give him greater access to her mouth. He framed her face with his thumbs on her cheeks and tasted her languidly with his tongue.

He swept his hands down her back and anchored her to him with his hands on her rump. Shifting around, he leaned back against the wall and pushed one of his legs between hers.

All his plans for a nice and easy seduction had gone out the window. He wanted her too much. When she arched her back, he pulled her more firmly into his body. He lifted his head and noticed her eyes were closed.

Carefully he brushed his mouth over both of her eyelids and then trailed his lips back to hers. He had to taste her again. He had a thirst for her that could never be quenched. A kind of thirst that had always been there. For the first time he felt he might be close to finding what he'd been longing for.

She was shorter than he was and smaller. She made him feel like a big he-man who could toss his woman over his shoulder and carry her off. And he really couldn't go to bed with her without telling her about the bet. He knew he couldn't go back to Stevie and say he'd changed his mind.

She pulled back and stared up at him with her eyes wide. He was pushing too hard and he knew it. The spur wasn't Stevie and that damned bet but the fact that he'd wanted her for so long. And she was still keeping him waiting.

"Still not afraid of me?" he asked. He didn't want her to be. He wanted to be able to figure out what role he had to play to win her. Not because of the money but because he felt good around Raine.

She shook her head and edged away from him. He closed his eyes and searched for that place he always found. That calm oasis that enabled him to forget to be the real Scott Rivers and instead play a role.

But it wasn't working. All he saw in his mind was Raine lying on his bed, her hair spread on the pillow, her small frame naked and her luscious curves bare to his touch.

"Scott?" she asked, her voice soft and pleading.

"Give me a minute," he said. His own voice sounded harsh and almost guttural, but having her in his arms was more than he'd expected. He made himself recite dialoguefrom his last action flick in his head until his body was at least a little back under his control.

"That got a little out of control," he said.

She rubbed her fingers over her lips. "You're right. I'm sorry…I can't do this."

"Do what?"

She shook her head. "Listen, no one on the tour is supposed to get involved, and that goes double for me and someone as high profile as you."

"Joel's not going to give a damn what I do. And I'm not really high profile." He didn't like that she was right. That she had a legitimate reason to back away from him. Why did she keep finding barriers for them?

"He's my boss and unlike you, rich boy, I need this job."

That made him feel like an insensitive cad. He knew he should have considered the implications to her job more carefully. And with Stevie already knowing he was after Raine…the complications were endless. He turned, grabbing her waist and pulling her back to him.

"Don't make me out to be some sort of spoiled celebrity with more money than compassion."

"Then don't act like one. Let me go."

"I don't want to. Not yet. I'm sorry for grabbing you like that but my hands are still tingling from touching you and I'm not ready to let go."

"Scott, don't toy with me. I'm not used to playing in your league and I'm not sure I know the rules."

"What rules?"

"The rules for affairs."

"Do people still have affairs?" he asked, toying with one of her curls.

"Did you want something more lasting?" There was something in her eyes he couldn't read. Something that made him feel like maybe this was a test and he knew in his gut that he wouldn't pass it. This was the normal-life thing he always screwed up.

Because he did want more with her. His instincts said take this woman and hold on to her. For how long he had no idea. But he knew he wanted her for the foreseeable future.

"That's what I thought. I'm not sure I want to risk my career for you."

This time, when she pushed against his chest, he let her go. She started down the hall and he followed her, watching that sexy ass of hers in those skin-tight-oughta-be-illegal jeans she was wearing. Damn, he'd screwed up and had no idea how to make this right.

"Dammit, woman, you need to buy some new jeans."

"What's wrong with these?" she asked.

"They are too damn tight." He had the feeling this wasn't winning him any points. But he knew he wasn't the only man to notice her ass, especially in those jeans.

"Stop cussing. That's a sign of low intelligence."

That stopped him in his tracks. He knew she was right. "I'm smart enough for you."

"I didn't say you weren't. Just that you were swearing too much."

"You bring that out in me."

"Makes me wonder why you're following me," she said, pausing in front of her hotel room door.

"I told you, I can't get you out of my mind."

"Not my problem, Scott."

"I think you're a chicken."

"That's not very mature, just because I don't want to have a… What did you decide we should call it?"

"We'll stick with your word."

"Just because I don't want to have an affair doesn't mean I'm scared."

"No, it doesn't. The fact that you run from everything that doesn't fit in your neat little life does."

She looked like she was going to smack him. He waited for it, knowing he'd pushed too hard and gone too far. But Raine needed someone who didn't accept the boundaries she laid down.

She swallowed and turned her key card over in her hand. "I… You might be right. But I can't deal with you and the possibility of losing my job."

"What if I square things with Joel? I'm doing this TV show as a favor to him."

"No. Please don't mention this to anyone. I think I'd die of embarrassment."

"Don't want to be seen with me?"

She bit her lower lip. "Don't want to be speculated about."

Scott knew then that he'd made a huge mistake in

letting Stevie goad him into making the bet. Raine was intensely private, and in a flash he knew that was why she'd given him such a difficult time. She wasn't sure how to handle him and the baggage he brought with him. No way was she ever going to understand why he'd made the bet. Right now Scott himself didn't understand what the hell he'd been thinking.

He reached out and tugged her into his arms, settling her so that her head rested against his chest. He wanted to make promises, the kind always made in romantic movies, but he knew he wasn't that sort of guy. And he knew that Raine would know the line for what it was.

"Take a chance on me, honey, and I promise you won't regret it."

Taking a chance on Scott was more tempting than she vowed he'd ever know. Tempting in the real sense. Tempting because she wanted to forget that he'd made a callous bet about her and really believe the lines he was feeding her.

She closed her eyes, slid her arms around his waist and just held him. The spicy scent of his aftershave surrounded her. His chest was solid, muscled. Not the chest of a pampered rich boy. She knew then that there was so much more to Scott than met the eye.

Was there more to the bet than she'd observed? She didn't know and in this moment she didn't care. She pretended for a moment that she wasn't the director of a television show that he was one of the stars of. She pretended that she wasn't the daughter of a gambler who knew better than to believe a man in the middle of a heady winning streak. Pretended that for once her luck had changed and this man was the fantasy, not the imitation she knew him to be.

In the distance she heard the elevator car ding. She stayed where she was until she heard voices heading their way. Sneaking around was a pain in the butt, but she wasn't sure enough of anything to risk her job. They couldn't afford to be seen together like this. Forget the con and the game she was playing, her job was on the line.

She pushed away from Scott. "Someone's coming. I've got to go."

She saw Scott narrow his eyes, and it bothered her that he knew she was trying to push him away so she could hide. She wished he'd let her get away with it. She glanced furtively down the hall. "The hiking was nice. Thanks for letting me drive your car."

He shook his head. "I want to finish our conversation and not be rushed away."

The voices were coming closer and she recognized one of them as Joel. "Please, Scott."

He smiled down at her so sweetly she almost believed him for a minute. Almost believed that he was real and genuine. "Anything, sweetheart, when you ask like that."

He ambled down the hallway and out of sight just as Joel walked around the corner with Andy, Raine's assistant director.

"Talk to you later, Joel," Andy said, entering the

room right next to Raine's. Her hands shook as she realized how close she'd come to getting caught alone
with Scott. Not that they'd been doing anything. Jeez,
did she have a guilty conscience or what?

"Got a minute to talk to me?" Joel asked as soon as
they were alone.

"Sure. Come in." She opened the door and let him
into the minisuite with separate sitting area.

Joel was in his forties, tall and handsome in a clas-
sical way. But underneath that boy-next-door facade
she'd heard rumors that he was a bad boy. She personally didn't see it but that could have had more to do with
the fact that Joel had always treated her like a little
sister.

"What did you want to talk about?"

He took a deep breath and walked over to the plate-
glass windows that looked down over the Vegas strip.
"I noticed you and Scott in the casino earlier."

"Uh, I can explain."

He held his hand up. "You don't need to. Just make
sure it doesn't go any further than flirting, Raine."

She nodded. Joel turned the conversation to business, but inside Raine was in turmoil. She was risking
everything she worked hard for and for what? To prove
something to Scott.

She wished that were true but she knew she was taking the risk because she genuinely liked him and he'd
hurt her. And right then she knew she'd made the wrong
choice. Whatever she'd intended, it wasn't worth it. The
afternoon spent with Scott had proved that she really

did like him, and if she spent any more time in his company she was going to fall for him.

Joel left a few minutes later, and Raine sank to the floor of her room, knees drawn up and her head resting on them. What was she going to do?

Her body still tingled with arousal from Scott's kisses. She wanted that man. It had nothing to do with his bet or her supposed con of him. And everything to do with body chemistry and sexual awareness. She wished for a minute that those reasons were enough for her to go to bed with him, but knew she couldn't do so until the taping wrapped up.

There was a knock on the door and she knew before she opened it that it would be Scott. She pulled him into her room before Andy opened his door.

"Did Joel talk to you?"

"Yes," she said, crossing to the small love seat that faced the windows and sinking down on it.

"What'd he want?"

"Nothing."

"Nothing?" he asked, sitting down next to her, so close she felt the heat of his body through the thin layer of her clothing.

She closed her eyes but that just made it worse. With every breath she took she inhaled his heady masculine scent. He stretched his arm along the back of the love seat and touched her face with just his fingertips.

She opened her eyes, surprised to see the concern in

his gaze as he watched her. "You're not a good enough actor to lie convincingly. I know he upset you. Tell me what he said."

She shook her head. She'd lied convincingly for the first twelve years of her life, and this man looked at her and saw…what? She didn't know. But he didn't see her past, and that warmed her deep inside.

"You can't fool a professional actor."

"I don't want to fool you. I just want to—"

He leaned over and put his fingers over her lips. They were warm and smooth. "Tell me what Joel said."

"He warned me to stay away from you."

"Ah, I thought that might be the case. What should we do? I have to be honest here, Raine, I don't want to let this end."

Because of the bet? she wondered. Was she really worth fifty thousand dollars to him? The thought of money changing hands because of her actions was abhorrent. She should call him on it.

Before she could say anything, he pulled her closer, wrapped his arms around her and just held her. No one in her entire life had done that. "We'll figure this out, sweetheart."

She blinked her eyes to keep from crying at the sweetness of the moment. She felt protected in his arms, something she'd never felt before, and she didn't want to lose that.

This was what she'd always hated about running a con. For her there was no easy switch off of the emotions needed to convince a mark that she was sincere.

And that kiss… Hell, that had had nothing to do with any kind of plan. That had been solely for herself.

That had been the kind of kiss she'd been wanting until she'd heard him making his wager with Stevie.

She looked at him. "Why are you here?"

He framed her face with his hands. She loved the way he did that. Got up close with her and made her feel…like she was special.

"I'm here because you intrigue me."

She pushed to her feet and moved away from him to the window. She stared out at the Vegas strip. Her room afforded her a view of the Golden Dream next door and the huge man-made waterfall that ran every half hour. She watched that, hoping it would make her remember that Vegas was all one big illusion.

Fake waterfalls instead of the real thing they'd seen at Red Rock. Nothing that happened here was real. Nothing that happened here translated into the real world. Even though this was her home for three weeks, next month she'd be in Glendale and back to her normal life.

He came up behind her, just stood there not touching her. She saw his reflection in the glass, noticed the way he watched her. "This is exactly why I came back to your room."

She didn't respond to that. She was used to freezing men out with her cold shoulder, but for some reason that didn't work with Scott.

"It's not going to work," he said as if she'd responded to him. "I'm not going to walk away from you, Raine. I think we have something worth exploring."

She turned to face him. "Then be honest. I'm not willing to risk everything for a guy who won't be honest with me."

Scott froze. Did she know more than she was letting on? Did she realize that he was the kind of man who always pretended to be whatever man would best fit the situation?

"That's easier said than done." He pushed his hands through his hair and took two steps away from her.

"You're asking me to take a big chance with you," she said.

When had life gotten so complicated? This was the first time he hadn't been able to glibly talk his way into what he wanted. His words, always his ally, deserted him. His body was on fire for her and he didn't care about anything but Raine. "I know. I just…"

"Expected to get by on charm?"

He had to smile at the way she said it. Because that was exactly what he'd expected. It should bother him that she knew him so well, but a part of him knew it was right that she did. Because he could see past her defenses, as well. "It usually works."

She smiled back at him, and he was reminded of how much he liked her spunk. "Maybe that's part of your problem. You're too used to getting your own way."

"Hello, pot, it's the kettle calling."

She threw her head back and laughed. His gut tightened, and arousal spread slowly throughout his body. His heartbeat accelerated as he remembered every essence of her kiss and how her body had felt pressed to his.

He wanted her. Whatever he had to do, whoever he had to be to make it happen, he would do it.

She tipped her head to the side, staring over at him. She licked her lower lip, and he wondered if she could still taste him. He wanted to taste her again. To just hold her in his arms on the bed and kiss her until he knew all the secrets of her mouth.

"Scott?"

"What?" he asked, knowing what he felt was revealed in his body. No matter how good he was at acting, there was no disguising his reaction to her.

"You're looking at me like…"

Like he wanted to toss her on that bed and make love to her all night. Even then he had the feeling he still wouldn't be sated. What he felt for Raine was too intense for one night to ever be enough. "Like a starving man looks at a tray of food."

She scrunched her face up and moved away from him, propping one hip on the small table that occupied the sitting area. "I'm not sure that's a compliment."

"How could it be anything else?" he asked, pacing toward her. No matter how close he got to her she was always dancing just out of his reach.

"If you're starving, anything would look good." she said, arching one eyebrow at him as if daring him to argue.

"Well, let's just say I've been in the grocery store, and nothing looks appealing except you."

"Scott, didn't your mama tell you not to say things like that?"

He knew his mom would kick his ass if she knew what he'd been up to in Vegas. He also sensed she'd really like Raine. Scott knew he had to figure out how to keep her, keep their secret and keep Stevie from being the wiser. "All she told me was women need to be told the truth."

"And that relates to the grocery store how?" she asked.

He glanced at his watch, knowing she had a job to do and probably needed to head out in a few minutes. But they had just enough time for one more kiss. "You're the only woman I see who attracts me, Raine."

"I'm not exactly model material."

He hid a smile. That was precisely why he wanted her. He liked the way she looked. She was fresh and unique, not enhanced by Botox or plastic surgery, just one hundred percent real woman. And she didn't act like other women did around him. She didn't treat him as if he was something special.

She treated him as she did everyone else. And that was telling. Unfortunately, she kept everyone at arm's length, but he was determined to find a way around her barriers.

"You are perfect the way you are."

"I wish I could believe you."

"It's easy. Just do it." The best way he knew to convince her that he wanted her—not just any other woman—was to take her in his arms. But he knew that she didn't trust that. That his reputation as a playboy was tripping him up here with her.

"If only I could. But I heard you with Latesha in makeup earlier."

"She's gorgeous and full of life. I love Latesha."

"I adore her, too, but I think your mirror might be off. We are nothing alike."

"Exactly. I'm not like every other man you've met before, honey. I see things differently."

"But how can you? You grew up in the land of the lovely people."

"That's why. I see past the perfection to the shallowness, the emptiness that is usually inside. Not in everyone. But I developed a way of finding out what was real."

"Tell me how you do it."

"Why?"

"So that I can use it on you."

"Honey," he said, moving closer to her. When she said things like that she broke his heart. He lifted her onto the table and stepped between her legs.

He tipped her head back and lowered his mouth to hers. He felt her hands at his waist and struggled to stay in control of his lust.

Her phone rang and she leaned around him to grab the handset. "Montgomery."

She listened for a minute, one hand caressing his chest while she talked. "I'll be right there. Sorry, I lost track of time."

She hung up and glanced up at him. "I've got to go. You cost me a shower, Rivers."

"I wish I'd known. We could have had our discussion in the bathroom."

"I bet," she said, pulling his head down to her. She bit his bottom lip then soothed it with her tongue. "You're not in charge of this."

She hopped off the table and headed toward the door. And like a man he followed her.

Five

Scott had spent the past four hours hanging with Hayden and watching him finesse the many whales in the casino. He'd hoped to find Stevie and call off the bet, but the rocker wasn't to be found. Once Shelby's lingerie shop in the hotel closed, Hayden disappeared and Scott watched his friend go. He'd never seen Hayden happier and more…he didn't want to say it, but alive. It was as if Shelby had given Hayden something he couldn't find on his own.

A big part of Scott wanted that. He wanted what Hayden had found, but he wasn't sure he wanted it forever. Over the course of his life "forever" had proved to be something rather short-lived. Something told him betting about taking Raine wasn't going to be conducive to finding the kind of relationship Hayden had.

He checked his watch and realized that Raine would be finishing up her editing session. Trying to be nonchalant, he cruised on by the editing suite and lounged against the wall, waiting.

Richard Weed, the show's main editor, emerged first. Nodding to Scott, he said, "You were a little off today."

Scott shrugged. He knew it was because of Raine. She wasn't the only one with job security issues. If he didn't figure her out he was going to probably get kicked off the game in the next few days.

He realized he'd made a huge tactical error in coming down here. Now another person from the crew had seen them together. "I need to talk to the director about the shoot tomorrow."

"Whatever, man, I'm out of here." He walked past Scott down the long hallway that led back to the main casino area.

A few minutes later Raine stepped out of the editing suite and paused. She'd pulled her thick hair back into a ponytail, and loose tendrils curled around her face. She had on a pair of tortoise-rimmed glasses that made her look adorable.

She pulled them off and rubbed the bridge of her nose as she studied him. After glancing up and down the hallway, she asked, "What are you doing here?"

"I wanted to see you again tonight. You feel up to a little gambling?"

"Not really, and Joel already caught us in the casino once."

"How about a walk down the strip? Nighttime is when you see the real Vegas."

She slung her backpack purse over her shoulder. "I don't want anyone to notice us."

"I know the back way out of the casino. Follow me."

"I want to see the strip. I'm thinking of including in each episode some live reaction from the people here."

"Good idea. But I was hoping that tonight we could just be Scott and Raine. I want to show you my world."

"Your world?" she asked.

He couldn't read her and he didn't like that. Usually her emotions played close to the surface; it was one of the things that drew him to her. "I spend as much time here as I do in L.A."

"Do you have a home here?"

"I have a place on Lake Henderson. When we wrap I'll probably head over there for a few weeks of down time. Want to join me?" he asked.

He saw her eyes narrow, and something came over her. Her body posture changed, and he knew something important had happened. But he didn't know what. Had he screwed up in that guy way again?

"Maybe. Let's see how these few weeks play out."

"You're very cautious. Why?"

"Growing up I was the sensible one. I guess it stuck."

Soon they were outside and he led them into the flow of traffic. Scott wanted to pull out his quirky guide role and entertain her with stories of his wild youth spent with Hayden MacKenzie, Max Williams and Deacon Prescott. The four of them had cut a wide swath through Vegas, gambling, drinking and living large with the ladies.

But it felt right to just slip his hand in hers and pretend they were like any other couple here. He knew that reality was going to rear its ugly head soon, but for right now, for just one more night, he wanted to pretend.

He also knew that in the morning he was going to confront Stevie and put an end to his bet. He had the feeling that Raine wasn't going to forgive him so easily.

She laughed at some of his stories, reprimanded him for some of them but by the time they were standing in front of the Mirage watching the water fountain show, she had her hand tucked into his and he knew he'd made some progress in wooing this very shy woman.

He ended with a story of how he and his friends had once gotten busted in one of the casino's luxury suites with six girls and too much booze. The story was funny because the women were from a church group in Arkansas and they were trying to reform the four of them. Alan MacKenzie—Hayden's dad—found them the next morning and was not pleased.

"So you got busted by Hayden's dad and then what?"

"He put us to work in the casino as dealers. But we enjoyed it too much so he switched us to the security detail. If you're really good I'll tell you how I busted a ring of dealers who were stealing from the till."

"Define *good*."

"Hmm, let's see. You could put your hand in my front pants pocket again and we could start negotiating."

"Do you always think of sex first?"

"With you, yes." Because he couldn't be honest with her about Stevie, he felt compelled not to lie about anything else. The only untruth would be that one. He knew it was a big one, but for some reason he felt better knowing he wouldn't lie anymore.

"I think you should have fudged on that."

"Why lie? I think it's obvious I want you."

She smiled at him then, and everything inside him clenched. She wrapped her arms around his neck and pressed her body against his. He felt her mouth nibbling softly against his neck as her hands slid down his back and cupped his behind.

Everything went on point. All day long he'd been waiting for this. Been waiting for her. And now he had her. He knew he had to handle this entire thing carefully because he was beginning to think he was more like Hayden and Deacon than he'd expected. He might be one of those guys who wanted to wake up every day next to the same woman. Not just any woman—Raine.

But that damned bet was going to cause him problems. Plus this was a role he wasn't sure of himself in. But with Raine in his arms he didn't want to think of anything except how her breasts felt pressed to his chest.

He slipped his hands under her T-shirt and felt the satiny smooth skin of her back. He traced his finger up the line of her spine and then back down again. He skimmed his fingernail along the edge of her jeans and wished he'd waited until they were somewhere semi-private before he'd started this.

She tipped her head back. "Was that good enough?"

"That was great. But not enough."

"Not for your story?"

"The story? What story?"

She laughed then, and he knew he was a goner. He was falling for her with each little thing she did.

Watching Scott made Raine realize that gamblers came in different forms. She'd never noticed before that there were different types. All she'd seen was the obsession to play and the fixation on the big score.

Her father was always promising big things when he hit the jackpot, so his gambling was always tied in her mind to money and their lack of it.

Of course, Scott was showing her his best side. But his stories showed her that some men gambled for the thrill of it. For the fun of pitting their skills against everyone else's and coming out on top.

"I want to hear the story about you busting a ring of dealers who were stealing from the casino."

"Ah, that one. Well, being in security is not as exciting as it might seem at first."

"It doesn't sound all that exciting to me."

"When you're a twenty-one-year-old guy it does." There was a sparkle in his eye that told her he'd had visions of being a cool undercover cop like Johnny Depp in *21 Jump Street*.

"Had you ever played a cop?"

"No, and I was ready to."

"Did you get a gun?"

"No, and that was only part of the disappointment. Alan put us all in the laundry area and had us watching over uniforms."

"I'm beginning to think Alan is a very smart man. I bet you all hated that."

"We did. Actually, Max and I talked about leaving. We didn't live in Vegas full-time, so we could have, but we didn't want to leave Deacon and Hayden to suffer alone."

"Why not?"

"Well, it was kind of my idea to try to convince the girls to give up their saintly ways."

"Why?"

"We had some idea of being a modern-day Rat Pack. Drinking, gambling and…"

"Womanizing?"

He shrugged and looked a little sheepish. "Keep in mind I was young."

She shook her head. "You had to pay the piper, so to speak."

"Yes, I did. Besides, Alan wasn't above calling my folks, and they thought I was a good boy."

She laughed. He made her feel good deep inside. And that was playing hell with her emotions. She wanted to be the cool grifter, playing up to him to gain his confidence and his affection and then turn it back on him. But she couldn't because he was unexpectedly more real than she'd ever thought he could be.

Deep inside that made her feel sad at what might

have been if Scott had been a different guy. Because he had something that drew her.

"After three days working in the laundry I noticed a pattern involving one of the baccarat operators."

"What kind of pattern?"

"He'd bring back the same uniform every day."

"Isn't that the point of the laundry?" she asked.

"Yes, smarty. But they were issued three pieces and he never brought back the other two."

"Okay, so now you're suspicious and are about to go all Columbo on him?"

"I was more Rockford than Columbo, honey. When my shift was over I went out on the floor and scoped him out. Just to see if I was right about the uniform."

"Were you?"

"Of course. He was wearing a different uniform. I watched him for a while before realizing that when he was putting the chips in the tray, he was pocketing a few each time."

"Did you make the bust then and there?"

"You're making fun and this was like a *COPS* moment."

"I see that. I can hardly wait to hear how you took down this embezzler."

"It wasn't that exciting. I waited until the end of his shift and confronted him."

"Wasn't that dangerous?"

"Nah, turns out he was a fan. When I told him I was reporting him to Alan, he didn't like me so much any-more."

There was something in his voice she couldn't place. A tone of almost sadness when he spoke. "Fans are fickle."

"They are. But that doesn't bother me. I was totally out of the business by that point. It was something he said."

"What'd he say?"

"That it was easy for me to turn him in because I didn't need the money and I wasn't living on the weekly check Alan was giving me."

That sounded like a first-class con to her. She'd heard her father use a variation of it every time he got busted for a scam. "Did you fall for it?"

"For about a second, but Hayden had seen me leave the floor and he followed me. He stepped into the fray, defending his old man and pointing out that the casino workers were the best-paid on the strip."

She slipped her hand in his and led him down the street toward the Chimera. She saw Latesha and a group of women from the makeup department coming out of the casino and wanted to get away before anyone saw them together. "Was your undercover work what you expected?"

"Yes and no. It wasn't very exciting. I wouldn't do it again. After we turned in the baccarat guy, he rolled over on three other employees who were doing the same thing. Two blackjack dealers and a girl in the cashier's box."

"Why did you notice the baccarat guy?" she asked.

"That's my game. I'm good at poker because I can bluff like nobody's business, but I really love baccarat."

"Why?" she asked, knowing that all gamblers had their game. They picked up skills at other games because they were in the casino all the time. She'd been starting to think that Scott was different because he didn't seem to be like her dad, but maybe she was wrong. Her gut instincts around gamblers were always a little messed up.

"It's complicated, and you have to really think while you're playing."

"Not everyone views it like you do," she said, more to herself than to him. But she easily pictured her dad, who was focused on winning, on the next big score, and only thinking of his strategy to win. Not about the outcome if he lost.

"How can you be sure? You didn't even know how to play roulette."

"I knew. I just didn't want to play. I know more about casinos and games than you'd expect."

He tugged them off the main path and into a quiet area just before the pirates' outdoor water show. "How? I know you aren't a gambler."

"No, I'm a gambler's daughter."

The Chimera had a small grill tucked away on the second floor. Scott led Raine there. Unfortunately, Richard and Andy were seated at one of the front tables, so Scott let go of Raine's hand.

"I'm going to sit in the back and wait for you."

She nodded to let him know she'd heard, and he walked past her, smiling at the hostess. He was seated at his usual table in the back, tucked out of the traffic and secluded.

Raine joined him almost twenty minutes later. She looked tired when she sat down on the banquette. He pulled her against his side. She didn't scoot away from him and instead leaned a little into him.

"What do you want to drink?" he asked.

"Decaf cappuccino, please."

He ordered two of them and a plate of biscotti, then put his arm around her. "Did they notice?"

"Yes," she said. "But I told them I had you show me some of your favorite spots and that I'm going to follow up with the other celebs. So tomorrow night you're going to have go out with the cameraman and show him 'your Vegas.'"

"I don't mind. I'm glad you came with me tonight."

"Me, too," she said, sipping her drink.

"Tell me about growing up as a gambler's daughter. Was it exciting always hanging around high-stakes gamblers?"

"I don't want to talk about it. Tell me another story about your escapades. Do you have any with Joel?"

"Yes, but I don't want to just talk about myself all night."

"Most guys do."

She kept pushing him into a neat little corner with every other man she'd ever met. He wondered why she did that. Was she really not interested in him? Or did she do it to protect herself?

"I'm not most guys. Now, back to you... Was it

Kenny Rogers in *The Gambler*, or *Fear and Loathing in Las Vegas?*"

"Do you use movies to relate to everything?" she asked.

He ignored her question. He did use movies to keep a distance between himself and others. And with Raine that was especially hard to do because he wanted to get it right. Not in the way that Hollywood did with their canned endings, but in the way that millions of people did every day in their private lives. And that was the one thing he'd never figured out how to get.

"What was your childhood like?"

"It's not a pretty story. I doubt that you with your charmed life are going to want to hear it."

He cupped her face in his hand, waited a few moments until he was sure she was focused on him. He couldn't change his past or his life. The truth was he'd known his share of tragedy, and he wasn't going to apologize for the successes that he'd had. The fact that he knew she was striking out at him to keep him from asking more questions about her past didn't mean he was willing to let her get away with it.

"That's not nice."

She turned her face in his hand, rubbing her cheek against his palm. "I know."

"Why'd you say it?"

She kissed the center of his palm. "I'm tired."

"So?" he asked, trying not to be affected by her mouth on his skin.

"I get mean when I'm tired," she said, putting her hand on his thigh.

"That was mean?" he asked. He could barely think with her so close to him. Raine couldn't be mean if she tried. She was too innocent of the real evil in the world. Even growing up with a gambler wasn't enough to taint her.

"Yes."

He cupped the back of her head and lowered his, tasting her mouth with long sweeps of his tongue. He didn't need to know about her past for this. He liked the way she felt in his arms. Liked the way she always opened for his kisses. Liked the way that she seemed to want him just as he wanted her.

He pulled back. Her lips were wet and swollen from his kisses, and her eyes were slumberous.

"Honey, you've got a long way to go to see mean. For the record, my life hasn't been all sunshine and happiness."

"I'm sorry for that, Scott. I was hoping that maybe someone had the kind of childhood that your sitcom portrayed."

"There were downsides to life, as well."

"I know that on a rational level but it's very hard to look at you and not feel resentful. Tell me something bad about being Scott Rivers."

"Why?"

"I want to know something that no one else does."

"If I do, will you tell me about your dad?" he

asked, because he felt her childhood held the key to who she was today.

"I don't like to talk about my dad. My childhood was a combination of *Leaving Las Vegas* and *The Grifters,* only my dad was in the Angelica Houston role."

The dark movie that portrayed a mother-daughter team who ran cons and left the bodies behind wasn't the happy image he wanted for Raine. But it explained a lot about why she kept such a distance between herself and everyone else.

"Being a con man doesn't make your dad a gambler." Con men shouldn't have families, Scott thought. He could easily imagine the hard life that Raine would have had with her father always scamming someone for money and then gambling it away.

"His first love is gambling. Everything he does in life is to make enough money to gamble."

"So you don't trust gamblers?" he asked. Because even though he didn't gamble for a living he had the soul of a gambler. He always wanted to bet on something or take a chance because the odds were low that someone else would. And he'd made a major bet on her.

"No, Scott, I don't."

Six

The next morning Scott didn't want to get out of bed for their 9:00 a.m. call. But he'd built his life around being a professional so he was on the set by 8:45. Raine was in the corner talking with the cameramen and her assistant director. Her hair curled around her shoulders, and he remembered the feel of it in his hands and the taste of her on his lips.

Only five players remained, and this morning he looked over at Brian's vacant chair. The guy had been the best poker player in the Southeast and had won his share of matches on the road, but this game was only for one week, and one mistake had cost Brian his spot at the table.

Scott didn't want to screw up. But his concentration

had been off all day. It was as if Raine had taken over every part of his mind. All he could remember was how right she'd felt in his arms, and he wanted to get her alone again so he could pursue that.

He'd tried to find a moment to speak with Stevie but the rocker was surrounded by groupies and his latest girlfriend, a wafer-thin model from Sri Lanka. She was funny as hell and didn't put up with any of Stevie's usual antics.

Scott tried to be unobtrusive as he watched Raine but walking away from her last night had been hard. And only the fact that he'd made that stupid bet with Stevie had enabled him to leave. What he'd learned of Raine the day before made it impossible for him to go through with the bet. He knew she'd never forgive him if she found out about it, and knowing Stevie, Scott figured the man would get drunk and blab it to the world before too long.

"Scott, you got a minute?"

He glanced over at Joel. "Sure."

Joel led him away from the bustle of grips and props people doing their jobs. There was something very stiff about Joel, and Scott had a feeling he was going to get the same warning Raine had gotten yesterday.

"Is this about fraternizing?" Scott asked before Joel could say anything.

"Yes and no," Joel said as he rubbed the back of his neck. "I know you did me a favor by agreeing to participate in the show, but you have to be careful with Raine."

"Has someone said something?"

"Yes. And Raine's not like the other women you've met in this business."

"You think I don't know that?"

"I'm not sure. All I know is that *you* aren't playing up to your normal game and *she's* distracted."

"Joel, believe me, man, if I could get my head in the game I would."

Joel laughed. "Just be careful. Both of you. This could blow up in your faces."

He nodded, and Joel walked away. Latesha signaled him to come to the makeup area. As he sat in the makeup chair, he thought over what Joel had said. No matter what, he knew he couldn't be the cause of Raine losing her job.

An approaching voice interrupted his thought. "I know you've explained it to me before, but makeup still looks girly to me."

Without looking, he knew it was Hayden. But he didn't feel like joking around with his friend. For the first time in his life things weren't coming easily to him and he wasn't sure of the outcome. He'd never failed when he put his mind to something, but the stakes had never been so high, either. "Are you saying I look like your wife?"

"I shoulda said sissy. Not girly. You can't compete with my wife."

"I'm heartbroken. How will I go on?"

"I imagine you'll turn to your alien lover," Raine said as she approached the two men.

She didn't smile and he wondered if Joel had been warning her away from him again. Probably. Damn, he should have been more circumspect, but he didn't want to have to hide their relationship, and he knew that they had one. Even Raine would admit to that. He couldn't let her go. If that meant he had to leave the show, so be it.

"Mr. MacKenzie, what brings you to our set?" she asked, checking her clipboard for notes.

"I was hoping to watch hotshot here in action."

"We'll be shooting in about forty minutes. You're welcome to stay."

"I've got a meeting but my wife might be free."

"Have Sal put her name on the list and we'll let her in to the taping. She'll have to sign a confidentiality form regarding who wins."

"No problem. Is my assistant taking care of you?"

"Yes, Sal is great."

She glanced over at Scott and he had the feeling she wanted to say something. "Scott, can I see you in the booth when you're done here?"

"Sure thing," he said. He wanted a few minutes alone with her as well.

"Thanks for making us feel so welcome here, Mr. MacKenzie. Scott showed me some of his favorite sights in Vegas last night and one of them was in your hotel. We're hoping to do a montage with that will include a few shots of those locations. Will that be okay?"

"Call me Hayden. My dad is Mr. MacKenzie. I'm sure that will be fine. I'll have Sal assign one of our managers to go with your cameraman."

"Thanks, Hayden. Goodbye, guys."

She nodded and walked away. He loved the way her worn jeans hugged her rump. He remembered the way her hips had felt under his hands the night before and wished he hadn't done the gentlemanly thing and walked away.

Hayden let out a low wolf whistle. Scott elbowed his friend.

"Her jeans are too damned tight," Scott said under his breath.

"No, they aren't. They're perfect. Say the word and Ms. Montgomery can be invited to dinner on Friday." Hayden adjusted the cuff links at his wrists. He had a way of doing things like that and making it look natural. Scott often imitated Hayden when he wanted to look like a real aristocrat.

"Shove off, Hay. I don't need your help with a woman."

"Sure you don't. I helped Deacon get Kylie," he said.

"Liar. You almost broke them up."

"Well, how was I to know women didn't like to be bet on?"

Yeah, imagine that. It was as if he didn't already know that women got royally ticked off when men did stupid things like that. Kylie was soft and sweet, not at all like Raine, who'd probably get some kind of revenge on him if he didn't come clean soon. "Did Kylie take the news hard?"

"You heard from Deacon. She married him and then left him a few days later. That's one mistake I won't make again."

"Did she forgive him?"

Hayden's BlackBerry beeped before he could say more. "Gotta run. I'll be in the casino later tonight if you want to hang out again."

Scott nodded and watched his friend walk away. God, he regretted that stupid impulse that had made him take a bet about Raine.

He went to find her. Seducing Raine without letting the world know what he was doing was going to be difficult. He had a certain reputation that was going to suffer if he played this the way she needed him to.

Scott rubbed the back of his neck as he rapped on the door leading to the director's booth. Losing his reputation was worth it, if it meant he'd get to keep Raine.

Raine wasn't sure what to do with Scott now that he was here in her domain. She'd had a vague plan of coming clean with him. Forcing him to admit to his bet and then maybe starting over with a clean slate.

"Hey, sexy lady, you wanted me?"

"Yes, I do," she said, reaching out and pulling him inside. "Are you miked yet?"

"No."

Good, she thought. She didn't want anyone else to hear their conversation. She'd thought of nothing but Scott all night long and felt restless and edgy this morning. If he lost the game today, then he wouldn't be working on the production any longer, and she could eliminate losing her job as one of the risks of having an affair with Scott.

"I saw Joel over there talking to you. What did he want?"

"Same as he did with you."

"I was afraid of that. What do you think your chances are of winning today?" she asked.

"I'm feeling lucky," Scott said, resting against the back wall of her little room, arms crossed over his chest.

"Like you did at the roulette table?" she asked, arching one eyebrow at him.

"Very funny."

"I thought so!"

He walked around the director's booth, fiddling with the soundboard, noting the monitors and camera angles. "Roulette is chance. Poker, on the other hand, is science. Care to try your luck at the poker table?"

She thought about it. At one time in junior high she'd won enough money during lunch to pay for a trip for her and her mom to New York City. But that was long ago. "No. I don't think I'm going to test my newfound luck. I want to be the one woman who can say she beat Scott Rivers."

"Do you want to see me lose?" he asked.

He stopped messing around with the equipment and turned to face her. She felt as if he wasn't sure what role to take in the booth. As if he was feeling her out to see how she was going to react.

"Not exactly, but it wouldn't hurt your ego to not win once," she said quietly. This was where she knew if she was really running a con, she'd have said something dif-

YOURS FREE!

You'll get a great mystery gift with your two free larger print books!

GET TWO FREE LARGER PRINT BOOKS!

YES! Please send me two free Harlequin Presents® novels in the larger print edition, and my free mystery gift, too. I understand that I am under no obligation to purchase anything, as explained on the back of this insert.

PLACE FREE GIFTS SEAL HERE

106 HDL EFZT   306 HDL EFUU

FIRST NAME	LAST NAME

ADDRESS

APT.#	CITY

STATE/PROV.	ZIP/POSTAL CODE

Are you a current Harlequin Presents® subscriber and want to receive the larger print edition?

Call 1-800-221-5011 today!

Please allow 4 to 6 weeks for delivery. Offer limited to one per household. All orders subject to approval. Credit or debit balances in a customer's account(s) may be offset by any other outstanding balance owed by or to the customer.

▼ DETACH AND MAIL CARD TODAY! ▼

(H-PLPO-03/06) © 2004 Harlequin Enterprises Ltd.

The Harlequin Reader Service™ — Here's How It Works:

Accepting your 2 free Harlequin Presents® larger print books and gift places you under no obligation to buy anything. You may keep the books and gift and return the shipping statement marked "cancel." If you do not cancel, about a month later we'll send you 6 additional Harlequin Presents larger print books and bill you just $4.05 each in the U.S., or $4.72 each in Canada, plus 25¢ shipping & handling per book and applicable taxes if any.* That's the complete price and — compared to cover prices of $4.75 each in the U.S. and $5.50 each in Canada — it's quite a bargain! You may cancel at any time, but if you choose to continue, every month we'll send you 6 more books, which you may either purchase at the discount price or return to us and cancel your subscription.

*Terms and prices subject to change without notice. Sales tax applicable in N.Y. Canadian residents will be charged applicable provincial taxes and GST.

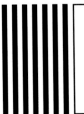

BUSINESS REPLY MAIL
FIRST-CLASS MAIL   PERMIT NO. 717-003   BUFFALO, NY

POSTAGE WILL BE PAID BY ADDRESSEE

HARLEQUIN READER SERVICE
3010 WALDEN AVE
PO BOX 1867
BUFFALO NY 14240-9952

NO POSTAGE
NECESSARY
IF MAILED
IN THE
UNITED STATES

If offer card is missing write to: Harlequin Reader Service, 3010 Walden Ave., P.O. Box 1867, Buffalo, NY 14240-1867 ferent. She'd have played up to him, making him feel like he was a god among men. Like Scott needed her to do that!

He tipped his head to the side and then said, "I've always been lucky in things of chance."

"What about love?" She didn't know why she asked the question except maybe it had been weighing on her mind. This had nothing to do with conning him and everything to do with the truth of what she felt. She was falling for him whether she wanted to or not. Last night she'd lain in her bed, frustrated and horny from reliving his kisses and wanting him there with her. What kind of lover—not physically, but emotionally—would he be?

"I think it's a draw when I'm dealing with love," he said in that wry tone that told her she was getting close to the truth.

"How so?" she asked, needing to know more. The rational part of her mind cautioned her heart not to get too attached to Scott. Not to fall for his openness and the way he really talked to her. A lot of money was on the line, and he just said he didn't like to lose.

"My folks are great. I have a few close friends who are always there for me. But when it comes to that one special woman…let's just say I've had my heart broken."

"Really?" She was surprised he admitted to it. She didn't know if she'd be brave enough to tell him about Raul Santiago, the young actor she'd had an affair with right out of college. She'd thought she finally had her life on track, with a new job as assistant director on a hot new television series, new boyfriend, new life. But Raul had really only been interested in her contacts, and once he'd gotten access to them, he'd moved on. No hard feelings, he'd said.

The sad thing was she hadn't had any feelings of remorse when he'd left. Maybe she was more like her father than she'd ever thought. He'd never seemed upset when he'd hurt her, nor when she'd left him the last time and told him she wasn't coming back. Of course, she'd still sent him money, so maybe he didn't care that he wasn't seeing her.

Scott replied to her question. "Yes. Want the gory details?"

Yes, she did, because she wanted to know what made him tick. Wanted to be sure she wasn't in over her head with a playboy who was really only romancing her for the money. "Would you really tell me? Aren't you afraid of looking like a loser?"

He laughed and smiled at her. "Honey, you keep a man humble."

"With you it's a real effort," she said. But it wasn't. He was a very natural guy.

"If you want to know about my heartbreak, I'll tell you. But only you. And maybe you'll feel sorry for me. I'm doing it for sympathy, not to seem pathetic."

"Ah, now I understand. Sorry, but I don't want to know about your past lovers."

He moved closer to her. The spicy scent of his aftershave teased her senses, and she wanted to breathe a little deeper so she'd always remember what he smelled like. She wanted to cuddle close to him and feel his arms around her again. The only time she'd ever felt safe was when he held her—and she knew that was dangerous.

"What about you? You ever get your heart broken?" he asked in that quiet way of his.

She didn't want to have this conversation. Not now. Not with him. She wanted him to believe she'd always been this calm, cool person he saw on the set. "Yes, more than once."

"Really? You strike me as someone who'd never let a man break her heart more than once."

"I'm not sure I like the sound of that. But you're right. It was only one man. The other times were my dad and my brother. You'd think I'd learn."

"Learn what?"

"Not to believe their promises."

"What do they promise?"

"To quit. To go straight. To live a normal life. You name it, my dad has probably promised it to me."

"So basically you've learned not to believe any promises a man gives you?"

"Basically."

"Well, then, I won't make you any promises," he said.

She couldn't respond, because she knew she wanted to believe the sincerity in his voice, the earnest look in his eyes that said he wanted to protect her: the promises that she wanted to weave around that unspoken one he'd just given her.

"What's the matter, honey?" he asked.

"Nothing," she said, not to annoy him, but because she didn't know how to say what she was thinking.

He closed the distance between them, wrapping his arm around her waist. She liked how he always touched her. She didn't analyze it, just snuggled closer to his solid chest. Closing her eyes, she pretended that they weren't on a television set and that this moment was real.

Seven

Scott held Raine in his arms, trying to remember that he could be a gentleman instead of a raving sex maniac. But he wanted her. Having her in his arms, feeling her curvy little body pressed against his was inflaming him. Driving out his good intentions.

Somehow he had a hard time reconciling good intentions and the bet he'd made. It would just take a few simple words to end his torment, but at this point he was in too deep to stop the train.

"I prejudged you because unlike Stevie, you don't have a real job."

He had a real job, but he kept it quiet. He knew it was better if everyone believed he was nothing more than a playboy. It enabled him to do his work without a lot of outside interference. "I run a charitable foundation."

"Really? I didn't know that. What do you do at the foundation?"

"I'm the CEO. That means I run the day-to-day operations."

"From a sound stage?" she asked in that snarky way of hers. She liked to push his buttons, and he was the first to admit he didn't mind it most of the time. But he was sensitive about his work.

"Or from my yacht or wherever I am in the world. I have a crack assistant who makes sure that I'm always up to date on whatever project we're working on."

"What are you working on now?" she asked.

He fiddled with the buttons on the soundboard in front of him. "A children's hospital in Orlando for low-income families."

"I'm impressed," she said, moving next to him and plugging in a pair of headphones.

He said nothing since this was the first time she actually sounded interested in something he did. Being a CEO was respectable. He knew it essentially involved being a number of characters rolled into one, based mainly on his friend Max Williams, who'd been running his own company since he was twenty-two.

"Nothing to say to that? I think I'm beginning to know you, Scott. You talk a lot when you're feeling… cocky, but if I get too close, you clam up."

"I think I know you, too," he said, not wanting to dwell on what she'd revealed.

KATHERINE GARBERA   103

He captured her wrist and held her hand against his chest. She scraped her fingernail down the buttons of his Oxford shirt. "I know you're a sleeping beauty, and it's going to take more than a kiss to get you out of your castle."

"Do you believe in fairy tales?"

"Yes, what about you?" he asked, because right now he had one in his head that went beyond a chaste kiss at the end.

"I guess. I'm surprised you do."

"What can I say? My mother is a literature teacher and she read me all kinds of stuff growing up."

"Including fairy tales."

"Hell, yes. And all kinds of women's fiction and nonfiction. She's a liberal feminist." Who'd be outraged if she knew her son had bet on a woman.

He turned away so that she couldn't read the guilty thoughts going through his head. He fiddled with the buttons on the panel again and accidentally pushed one this time. Voices filled the sound booth.

"Last night I saw them come into the restaurant together but then they separated." He recognized Andy's voice.

"I think it's kind of sweet if they are getting together."

Raine gasped. "Oh, my God. They're talking about us."

Scott hit the button again, tuning out the talk, and turned to face her. "How was that possible? Andy's not miked, is he?"

"The entire room has microphones in it, so we can

pick up different audio tracks and edit out what we don't need."

Had she heard him that morning with Stevie? He glanced over at her, watching carefully. He should tell her now. Apologize before things went any further, and make sure she knew he'd never meant the bet to be anything other than a bit of fun.

"Have you ever heard anything you wished you hadn't?" he asked, not sure how to broach the subject of his bet.

"I just did," she said. "I knew this wasn't going to work out."

"Why not? They were just speculating. We haven't done anything to be ashamed of."

She pushed past him and out of the booth and looked at that button and then down on the floor. Andy was standing right where he and Stevie had been the day they'd made their bet. The tightening in his gut said she had to know.

Nothing went right on the set once the entire cast and crew were there. Laurie Andrews kept throwing up, and the doctor they brought in ruled out food poisoning, telling Laurie instead that she was pregnant. The news was a blow to the woman and she asked for the rest of the day off to adjust to the news.

To top it off, Scott's discovery in the booth early this morning was just what she didn't need. Now she knew he had to guess she'd overheard the bet. Or maybe he was hoping she hadn't. But the time for silence was coming to an end. She needed to say something, and soon.

They were on a tight schedule that allowed for no extra days, and after a quick chat with Joel it was decided that they couldn't just give her the day off. Raine did, however, call a cut to taping and asked everyone to return after eight this evening. Laurie was okay with this as were most of the other players.

She spent an hour with the crew giving them some additional direction for things she wanted done this evening. She asked one of the cameramen to go get some exterior shots of the hotel. Once Sal got clearance from Hayden, which took another twenty minutes, she sent Stevie with the cameraman to show him some of his favorite okay-for-television spots in Vegas. Then finally everyone was gone and she was alone on the set.

For the first time in her life being alone felt lonely. She wished that she could go find Scott and spend some time with him, but people were talking about them and she knew she had to nip any gossip in the bud. She shrugged on her backpack purse and headed out toward the lobby.

As she neared the front door, she noticed Scott talking to a group of people. He broke away from them as she approached.

"What are you doing?" she asked as he approached her. She glanced around.

"Waiting for you."

Maybe she wasn't so alone anymore. He was starting to like her, and a big part of her knew that it was good for her con to sucker him in. But her heart treasured the fact that he seemed to like her for her.

"If you don't have plans, I'd like to take you for a ride on my Harley."

"I'm not sure that's such a good idea."

He nodded as if he understood some great universal truth. "Are you nervous about being seen or being alone with me?"

"Why would I be nervous about that?"

"Because we're not going to be around the casino where you're distracted and we're interrupted. I'm talking about you and me alone for the day."

To be honest it sounded like heaven, and for the rest of the day she was just going to try to forget about bets and men and gambling. "You can get a little tedious, so maybe I should think about this."

He snagged her close with an arm around her hips. "That sassy mouth has just landed you in a boatload of trouble."

"Wow, really? What are you going to do, spank me?"

"Maybe," he said, taking her hand and leading her out of the lobby and to the garage.

Her mind was full of images of herself over his lap while his hand came down on her naked backside. It was a little kinky and nothing she'd ever done in real life but it definitely aroused her.

He took her backpack and put it in one of the saddlebags on the bike and handed her a helmet.

She took it as she climbed on the bike like it was

second nature. Like he hadn't just thrown down a gauntlet she wasn't sure she was ready to pick up. But Raine knew better than to show any sign of weakness.

Normally she knew better. With Scott she just wanted to stop hiding who she really was.

"Want to see my place on Lake Henderson?"

She knew he was asking for more than just a trip to see his place and she took a deep breath and acknowledged that she was way beyond running a con on this man. She wanted him with the kind of soul-deep intensity she'd hidden from all her life. She was so afraid to believe in Scott.

So afraid that the pattern of her life would repeat itself. So afraid that she was going to look like a sucker who knew better than to take the sucker bet.

"Honey, what can I say to make your answer the one I want to hear?"

"Tell me that this isn't just some easy lay for you."

He cursed under his breath and turned away from her for a minute, on his head bowed. She knew that her words had affected him—more deeply than she'd intended.

"Dammit, woman, you are more trouble—"

"Than I'm worth?"

He turned to her. "Did I say that?"

"No, but I know I'm a bit of a shrew."

"Honey, I know better than to agree with that. No matter what you might have heard I'd never treat you that way."

Was he talking about normal gossip or hedging his

bets in case she'd overheard him and Stevie? It was too difficult to figure out, and since she wasn't supposed to know about the bet, she had no idea what to say to him. He stared at her for a minute before turning away again.

She climbed off the bike and walked over to him, put her arms around his waist and rested her head against his shoulder. "I'm not good at these kinds of things. I want to go with you but I'm not sure I'm ready."

His hands settled over her wrists, his callused thumbs rubbing over her skin. "Honey, I'll take whatever you're ready to give me. Hell, I'm more turned on by the thought of you riding pressed against my back than I am by the thought of taking any other woman."

She squeezed him tight. "Then let's go see this house of yours."

She dropped her arms and struggled to get the helmet on. Scott took it from her and put it on. "There. Now you're ready and no one will recognize you."

She was touched that he'd remembered she didn't want anyone to see them together. It was probably nothing to him but it meant something to her. He put on his own helmet, and then they both climbed on the bike, heading out of town, leaving the artificial world of Vegas behind and heading into the real-life world of Lake Henderson.

Raine clung tight to Scott's back and let her mind drift away from reality as she knew it. It had been so long since she'd just let herself go and relaxed with a man she truly liked. She was claiming this day for herself. She knew there'd be a price to pay later. But for now she was going to simply enjoy being with Scott.

Scott's house was built to take advantage of the view of the lake offered by his property. The entire back of the two-story structure was made of wood beams and glass. There was a deck leading to a pool and then a walkway down to the lake. He had a small boathouse where he kept a Bayliner, two Sea-Doos and a catamaran.

Raine had said little on the drive here and now that they were standing in his living room he wasn't sure what to say to her.

"I like this place. It seems a little rustic."

"Thanks. This is my place. I don't let anyone else come here."

"You brought me to your retreat?"

"Yes. We needed privacy, and no one has ever found me here."

"Thanks, Scott."

"Anything for my lady."

"My entire house would fit in your living room."

"I bet it's cozy."

She laughed and he smiled to hear it. "Point taken. I wasn't expecting this."

"What were you expecting?"

"I don't know…some cold, aesthetically pleasing house that looks like no one lives in it. But this is comfortable. I could sit in here, put my feet up and not feel out of place."

He was glad. He wanted her to relax and to drop her guard, which she never did. He opened the glass doors, pushing them into the pocket so that they were open to the outdoors. "Want to take a walk?"

"Just a walk? Isn't that too tame for you?"

"Keep talking, honey, that mouth is going to do you in."

"I don't think so. You like it when I tease you, because everyone else takes you too seriously. They're always trying to please you or flatter you to win your favor."

"But not you," he said.

"No, not me. I'm not wowed by your fame or your millions."

She made a circular route around the living area, stopping to study the pictures on the wall. Two of them were by an artist friend of his who was just starting to make a name for himself in the art world. They were bold landscapes that reminded the viewer that Mother Nature—not man—was still in charge of the earth.

"Who is this?" she asked. She reached out to touch the canvas but stopped.

"Thom Jenner. We're not in a museum. You can touch it if you want to."

But she didn't reach out. She kept her hands by her sides, very much the cautious woman she'd always been. "I've never heard of him. I think I'm afraid to touch it. The storm looks so real."

Scott walked over to stand next to her. "You will be hearing Thom's name soon. He's starting to make it big.

I picked up the *Grand Canyon* when I was in Denver last year." The *Grand Canyon* showed New York City being buffeted by a massive storm. The storm was definitely what drew your eye.

"Why do you have his work in here?" she asked. "What drew you to it?"

He considered her question for long minutes, studying the painting, trying to pick through his true reactions and decide what to tell her. Baring his emotions didn't fit with his role this afternoon—leading man in a romantic comedy. Light, sexy, funny. But Raine always reacted to the unexpected.

"You have to promise not to leak this to the media."

She held her hand up. "I solemnly swear."

"Well, I like that it takes symbols of what we consider successful and makes them seem small. It reminds me every time I see it that there's a lot more to the world than just big cities and—you'll love this—money."

She slipped her arm around his waist, sliding her hand into his front pocket the way he'd asked her to do that day in front of the elevator. "That's—"

"What?"

"Deeper than I expected of you. I think I glimpsed the real Scott under the role you've been playing."

He wrapped his arm around her shoulder, holding her to him as they stood under the painting. "I don't know if there is a real Scott."

Her eyes softened and she looked up at him like he was some kind of hero. And he never had been. He wanted to warn her that there wasn't any substance to him. That he'd always been an image on celluloid. Nothing more.

"There is. He's a nice man."

"Nice? I brought you here to seduce you."

"And that's not nice? Are you going to have your wicked way with me?"

"Yes. And then I'm hoping you'll have your wicked way with me."

She slipped her hand deeper into his pocket, edging it toward his inner thigh. She stroked her fingers against him, and his body responded. He tried to adjust his stance, glancing down at her to see that she was watching him harden in response to her touch.

Her other hand came up to lightly rub over his fly, and he groaned deep in his throat. She toyed with the tab of his zipper, glancing up at him.

"Can I?"

He was so hard and ready for her touch. "I think I'll die if you don't."

She popped the snap at the waistband of his jeans and then slowly lowered the zipper. She pushed her hands into his pants and ran her fingers over his length, still encased in the fabric of his boxer briefs.

"I'm ready to be seduced," she said, running her fingers over him.

Her hands were cool, her long fingers slipping inside his underwear to wrap around him. A drop of moisture leaked out, and she rubbed her finger over it, smoothing it into the head of his erection. He groaned at how good she felt with her hands on his body.

He realized he'd already been seduced by Raine in a way that had nothing to do with sex and everything to do with acceptance. He pulled her hands from his body, scooped her up in his arms and carried her down the hall to his bedroom.

This was where they both belonged. Far away from the bright lights of Vegas with its spinning wheels, gamblers and games of chance. Far away from the prying eyes that would threaten her career. Far away from everything except the real world he'd never thought he could really live in. But with Raine in his arms, he felt real, and that was enough for now.

Eight

Scott lowered her to her feet next to the bed. Raine realized that her con had ended probably that first afternoon on the desert trail in Red Rock. She knew herself well enough that she had no doubts about being here with Scott now.

"Take off your shirt for me, honey."

Her fingers trembled as she brought them to the hem of her shirt and lifted it to expose her belly button and the bottom of her ribs. "What makes you think you're in charge?"

He scratched his chin, studying the smooth skin she'd revealed. He reached out and rubbed his palm over it, and she shuddered at his touch, wanting more of it. She wanted his caresses all over her body.

"You're always in charge on the set. Don't you want to let go now?"

She did, but not because of that reason. She wanted to let go because she was afraid she'd do something to ruin this wonderful moment. That somehow with the same bad luck she'd always had she'd say the wrong thing and drive him from her.

"No, I don't want to be in charge," she said, her voice sounding husky to her own ears. The last time she'd had sex had been hurried and a way of saying goodbye to Raul. It had been emotionally painful. She hoped she wasn't setting herself up for a bigger heartache with Scott.

"Do you want to be mine?"

She thought about it, forgetting everything except the two of them together now. She remembered the feel of his body in front of hers on the Harley. She remembered his hand in hers at Red Rock. She remembered his face in front of the Bellagio hotel. She nodded.

He cupped her face in his hands and kissed her, his mouth moving tenderly over hers, his tongue dipping inside to taste her. "Say it out loud so there will be no doubts later."

"I want to be yours."

He ran his thumb back and forth over her lower lip. "And you'll do whatever I ask of you."

She hesitated. She wasn't really adventurous when it came to sex. "I'll try. What are you planning? I think you should know I'm strictly a missionary-position girl."

"We're going to expand your horizons a little. But only if you agree to do what I ask."

This was it. She took a deep breath and nodded. "I agree."

He kissed her deeply and quickly and then stepped back. He crossed his arms over his chest and surveyed his room. The windows had no coverings and looked out over the lake. She realized as she studied them that they were actually sliding doors that opened onto a deck.

"Does exhibitionism excite you?"

"Not today."

He nodded. "Then come away from the windows. Now, take your shirt all the way off," he said, walking across the room to the ladder-back chair in the corner. He moved it to the center of the room and sat directly in front of her.

She pulled it the rest of the way off and tossed it on the floor at his feet.

"Pick up your shirt, fold it and place it on the dresser."

She arched one eyebrow at him but did as he asked. She felt more vulnerable than she'd expected being almost naked from the waist up. She took heart in the fact that his jeans were unfastened and she could see his hard length through the opening.

"Now you," she said.

He considered her request for a moment then stood up and unbuttoned his shirt, revealing his sculpted chest. He had the best chest she'd ever seen. And the fact that he was here in this room with her—hers to touch and caress—made her wet.

She stepped closer and ran both of her hands down

his chest. The light dusting of hair was tingly against her fingers.

"Who said you could touch me?" he asked in that dominant tone of his, but his pupils were dilated and his pulse beat visibly at the base of his neck, so she knew he liked it.

"I can't?" she asked, skimming her fingernail down the center of his body. His stomach clenched and she slid the tip of her finger into the waistband of his briefs, touching the tip of his erection.

He put his hand over hers, moving her hand down his length and wrapping her fingers around him. He tightened his grip almost painfully on her hand and then drew her touch from his pants.

"Not yet. Take off your bra."

"Scott—"

"We both agreed I was in charge. Remove your bra so I can see your pretty breasts."

She reached behind her back and slowly removed her bra. Scott's breath caught in his chest and she watched a flush spread over his chest. His erection strained against the front of his underwear and his hands were clenched at his sides as he waited to see her.

Teasingly she tossed the bra at him. He caught it and put it on the dresser behind him.

"Offer your breasts to me, Raine."

A shiver of excitement pooled in her belly. She ran her hands upward from the waistband of her jeans to her breasts, cupping them. Watching Scott for his reaction. He groaned and unclenched his fists.

He reached out and ran his forefinger along the edge of her hand, right where her fingers cupped the globes of her breasts. Her nipples tightened, begging for his attention. He circled her aureole with just the tip of one finger.

He leaned down and licked the tip of one breast, sucking her deep into his mouth. She let go of her breasts and held his head. Held him to her.

Wrapping both of his arms around her waist, his mouth never leaving her nipple, he picked her up. He bit lightly at her nipple and let it go. It tightened painfully when the cool air touched it.

She shivered, staring down at him. He lowered her until the tips of her breasts rubbed against his chest. She sighed at the feeling. She wanted more. She wanted his mouth on her again.

"Wrap your legs around my waist."

She did, adjusting her body over his hardness and then rocking against him. He felt so good, and it had been a long time since she'd had sex. Everything in her focused on that contact through their jeans. His erection and her wetness. She held his shoulders and rocked harder against him.

"Wait," he said, holding her still. He set her on her feet, unfastening her jeans. He pushed her jeans and panties down her legs. He knelt at her feet to remove her shoes.

"Lift your feet, honey," he said in a deep rasp that she made her body clench.

She lifted first one foot than the other and soon she was standing naked over him. He ran his hands up the outside of her legs, his fingers slowly caressing every inch of her.

"Spread your legs."

She stepped her feet apart.

His hands moved to the inside of her legs, starting slowly at her ankle, lingering behind her knee and then sliding up her inner thighs. Her own moisture coated the very tops of her inner thighs; he rubbed his finger in the wetness there.

"Want me?" he asked.

"You have no idea."

He teased the opening of her body, circling his finger just at the rim, not entering her. She canted her hips forward, hoping to force him inside. But he moved his fingers away.

"Part yourself for me."

She did as he asked and felt his warm breath and then the brush of his tongue on her most intimate flesh. She trembled as he continued to caress her, and then her legs gave way. Scott supported her with an arm wrapped around her thighs and continued his intimate kiss until she was shuddering in his arms as her climax approached.

"I'm going to come," she said.

He pushed one finger into her body and then a second, thrusting them in and out of her while he scraped his teeth along her body. Everything inside her centered there where he was touching her, and her orgasm rocked through her. She grabbed his shoulders, held on to him while the world tilted and drifted away from her.

He lifted her and carried them both to the chair. He

sat down and she straddled his hips. His jeans abraded her inner thighs. She reached between their bodies and freed him from his underwear.

He was hot and hard in her hand. A drop of fluid glistened on the tip. She soothed it with her finger, rubbing it into the head of his erection, then lifted her finger to her lips and licked it.

"Did you like tasting me?" she asked.

"As much as I'm going to like taking you," he said. He set her on her feet for a minute then shucked his jeans and underwear in one fluid movement.

But they got caught on his boots. Raine eyed his erection; he was bigger than she'd realized.

She touched his shoulder and he looked up at her. She'd never wanted a man's body inside her as badly as she wanted Scott's at this moment. He pushed to his feet and sat on the chair. He had a condom packet in his hand.

He tore it open and donned it quickly. "Come here, honey. I need you."

She climbed on his lap and immediately felt too intimate with him. From this angle they were face to face. His eyes were open, staring into hers. His erection pressed between them, hot and hard, ready for her. And she was ready for him.

She closed her eyes and grasped his shoulders as he positioned himself between her legs. His hands moved to her hips and then swept up her back, cupping the back of her head. She opened her eyes and found him watching her.

"Ready?"

She nodded. Despite being in the position of power, she felt powerless. It had nothing to do with Scott and everything to do with her. She didn't like it.

The tip of his body was lodged in hers, and she bit her lower lip and slowly sank down on him. He groaned deep in his throat.

She held on to his shoulders and rocked against him. He let her set the pace. His mouth trailed over her shoulders and down to the curves of her breasts. She held him to her, scored his skin with her nails and rocked a little harder against him. But she wanted to see his weakness. She wanted to arouse him and then hold him at the point of orgasm.

She wanted to make sure that he was at least as vulnerable as she was in this affair of theirs.

The chair creaked as she increased her thrusting. Everything was building inside her to that glorious slide once more. Scott braced his feet on the floor and started thrusting up into her. His hands were no longer caressing but held her still for his thrusts. She found his mouth with hers.

She thrust her tongue into his mouth as his hands tightened on her hips and he grunted with the force of his orgasm. He thrust into her two more times and as her own climax rolled through her body, she sank deeper onto him.

She wrapped her arms around him and laid her head on his shoulder. He felt right in her body, holding her tight to him. She felt as if she'd found something she didn't know if she could ever give up.

That scared her because she knew that she wasn't running a con. In fact, she now saw she hadn't been from the beginning. What she'd been doing was trying to avoid falling for a man who could hurt her.

Why was she having this revelation now?

Scott carried Raine to the bed and set her under the covers. She rolled to her side, her eyes sleepy looking as she watched him remove his boots and then his pants. He went to the bathroom to dispose of the condom and then returned to his bed.

"When do I get to have my wicked way with you?" she asked, trailing her fingers down his chest. She slipped her hand between his legs and cupped him.

"What'd you have in mind?" he asked. He had a driving need to possess her. To ensure that she didn't take a breath that wasn't filled with his scent. That she didn't lick her lips without tasting him. That she didn't close her eyes without seeing his face.

"Well, since you were so big on orders I thought about ordering you around a little," she said. She stroked her hand up and down his erection in just the right way, squeezing him at the tip, then caressing down to his root and lightly teasing his scrotum with her fingers. She repeated the caress until he was harder than he'd ever been.

He raised one eyebrow at her. He toyed with the edge of the sheet, pushing it down her body until all of her curves were revealed. "I'm not sure that's a good idea."

"Why not?" she asked, still stroking him.

He could hardly think. He wanted to push her legs apart and thrust into her, but he wasn't sure she was ready for him again. "Because I like to be in charge in bed."

"So?" she asked, moving her hand to his erection. He sucked in his breath, painfully aroused and past the point of thinking.

He pushed her thighs apart and dipped one finger into her body. She was wet and hot, ready for him. He fumbled in the nightstand, finding a condom and handing it to her.

"You rode me last time, I'd say you were in charge."

She ripped open the condom packet and rolled it down his length. "Yes, but you were the one giving the orders."

He rolled her gently to her back and settled himself over her.

"Just like you're in charge this time?" she asked, bracketing his hips with her thighs.

"Exactly," he said. He reached between their bodies to adjust himself, then slid into her body. She felt so good around him; he wished he didn't have the condom on so he could feel her heat on his flesh.

She skimmed her fingers down his back as he thrust lazily into her body. She cupped his butt and moved lower, teasing his scrotum and pressing into the flesh beneath. His erection throbbed. He needed to get deeper. Now.

He crushed her mouth under his and started to thrust

harder, deeper. She continued her teasing play between his legs, and he realized he was going to come in a few seconds. He reached between their bodies and found her bud, stroking it with a few touches until he felt her body begin to tighten around his and he gave over to his orgasm.

Sweat coated both of their bodies, and he rolled to his back, tucking her to his side and holding her tight. The condom needed to be disposed of but for this moment he needed to hold her.

"Wow, I guess you showed me who was boss."

He leaned over and kissed her hard on the lips. "You have my permission to do that any time you want."

She laughed and he held her for a few more minutes before getting up to deal with the condom. When he returned to the bedroom she was staring out the windows at the lake.

"That was incredible. You are one hot lady."

He liked seeing her there, his blue sheets tucked around her bare limbs, her hair loose and hanging to her shoulders as she watched him and teased him. Raine was so perfect for him sometimes it scared him. She was yin to his yang and he didn't know if he could ever let go. He also realized there was a very real possibility that she might leave him when she found out how callously he'd behaved before ever really getting to know her.

He had to bind her to him. He'd use sex and charm, everything he had in his arsenal to make her fall for him before he had to tell her the truth, because this was the kind of thing that was going to hurt.

She was the first woman he'd had at this place. She was more precious to him than he could ever explain. Even thinking about it made him feel edgy. When he was with Raine, he never found the right role to play.

Being submissive to her will wasn't one he could slip into. It went against his grain and his true personality. He could pretend to be congenial with everyone else but not with her.

"Well, I do have my reputation to consider," she said and glanced away from him as he climbed in beside her.

He realized he'd said the wrong thing. "Dammit."

"What?"

"Just when I think it's okay to be myself I screw it up."

"What are you talking about?"

He rolled over, settling her underneath him. "When I'm not playing a role, I don't say the right things."

She reached up to run her fingers over his face. Though her touch was so light, he felt it all the way down his spine. It was the kind of caring touch he seldom experienced in bed. Most women were after the playboy Casanova and not a gentle lover. But with Raine he felt she really did see him. Both the good and the bad parts.

"Everyone screws up. That's what makes us human and real. This affair of ours isn't a Hollywood script."

"I know that," he said, settling beside her on the bed once more. That was the thing that scared him. He had a hard time creating lasting bonds away from the set.

He had no idea how to be the real Scott Rivers, and for Raine he wanted to be a good man. A real man. The kind of man she'd never had in her life. Not a gambler or a rogue, and those were the roles that came easiest to him.

He knew that the easy things in life weren't the ones worth having. Hadn't his parents said the same thing to him many times? Only now did he understand what they'd meant.

Nine

Back on the set Raine concentrated on work. Scott had left her at the garage elevator, and she'd gone back to her room to shower and change. Her assistant director, Andy, was already on the set when she got there.

"How's Laurie?"

"Good. Her boyfriend is flying out and they're going to get married at the end of shooting."

"I'll talk to Joel about taping it. Maybe we can get the show to pay for part of it."

"I thought you'd say that, so you're meeting with Joel tonight after taping. I also spoke to Sal on the QT and he said the Chimera would do something for her, as well."

"Great. Sounds like a nice bonus for our viewers."

They finished their discussion and Andy left to check on the players over in makeup. Raine went back to her booth to watch everyone taking their seats. Scott smiled up in her direction but did nothing else to even hint that they'd spent the day together.

By the end of the night, Junior McMillan, the NASCAR driver, was eliminated from play. It was almost eleven and Raine still had her meeting with Joel as well as post work to do.

When she exited her booth, she saw Scott in a corner speaking quietly with Stevie. She wished she could hear what they were saying. Was he collecting his bet?

She felt small and vulnerable thinking about it and as she turned to hurry away, she walked straight into the man behind her. His arms steadied her.

"Thanks," she said, looking up into the steel gray eyes of her executive producer and boss, Joel.

"You're welcome. You okay?" he asked.

"Fine. I just remembered something I'd forgotten. I was on my way up to see you," she said, needing to get the topic to business and not her dismal personal life.

"I thought I'd save you the trip upstairs since you'd probably be back down here editing when we were finished."

She smiled at him. "You know me well."

"We can talk in the edit bay," he said.

She led him out of their temporary sound stage and away from Scott. They walked down the short hallway to the room they'd set up as their editing bay while they were in Vegas. They discussed Laurie and her impending wedding and decided that they couldn't pay for any of it because they didn't want to seem as if they were partial to one player.

"We can shoot some of it and air it if she wins, but only after the fact. Maybe in the postmortem at the end of the episode," Joel said.

Each player had one-on-one camera time to discuss why they thought they'd lost the game.

Joel continued, "If she loses we can play the angle of how she might not have been lucky in cards tonight but she struck gold in love, marrying her longtime sweetheart, blah, blah, blah."

"Sounds good, except you're not the type of guy who can carry off 'blah, blah, blah.'"

"I know, I'm too stuffy."

"I wouldn't say stuffy."

"Not to my face."

She laughed. He was very different from Scott and for a moment she wondered how the two men had met and become friends. "That's right, not to your face."

With a hand on her elbow Joel drew her to the side and looked around. His expression grew serious, and her stomach sunk. She knew she wasn't the type of woman to sleep with a man and not have it get out.

"Was there something else?" She was almost afraid to ask.

"Yes. One of the stringers I know at the *Enquirer* said that a woman was photographed at Scott's Lake Henderson house."

She blanched.

"I wanted to let you know before it leaked out."

Did he know she was the woman or was he trying to save her some heartache? "I know."

"You were the woman." He said it without question in his voice.

"Yes."

"Dammit."

"Do you want me to resign?"

"Let's wait for the pictures and see if you can be identified."

"Why?"

"Because I like you and you're good at your job. And I think maybe you and Scott could be good for each other. To be honest I've never seen him this way with a woman before."

It was on the tip of her tongue to ask if he'd ever known Scott to risk fifty thousand dollars on a woman. But she didn't. Instead, they parted ways. Joel had a late-night game with some friends.

She drifted through the casino but didn't want to go up to her room yet. She didn't want to close her eyes and dream about Scott. She wasn't sure which Scott to believe. The one who'd held her so close to his naked body or the one who'd been in quiet conversation with Stevie.

She exited the hotel and walked on one of the many garden paths around the pool. There was a maze with a gazebo in the middle of it and she thought she might try to find that and…hide. But she couldn't hide from herself.

"Is this a private walk or can I join you?"

Scott. He was standing quietly in the shadows behind her. She couldn't see his features or anything except for his jeans-clad legs. She wasn't sure she was ready to talk to him.

She should have called him on the bet a long time ago instead of playing a game with him. Shoulda, woulda, coulda, she thought. You can't go back and change the past.

"I don't think that's a good idea," she told him. "Have you talked to Joel?"

"No, why?"

"He heard that the *Enquirer* is going to be running a picture of you and an unnamed woman taken at your place on Lake Henderson."

"Damn. I'm sorry, Raine. I never meant for that to happen. I'll call my lawyers and see if we can get the photo pulled."

"Can you do that?"

"I'm sure as hell going to try."

The grounds were mostly deserted; all the serious gamblers were inside the casinos playing their hearts out. The tourists were in their beds sleeping, since all the late-night shows were over. She felt as if she and Scott were the only two people here. But she'd thought that at the lake, too, and it had proved to be wrong. It was too late to just walk away. The damage had been done to her career. If anyone recognized her, she'd be fired from the show.

She wished they were really the only two people here. But instead she remembered seeing him earlier with Stevie, and she found that little girl deep inside her who'd learned how to play the game of the grifters. She knew what she had to do—hide her aching heart and lead Scott down the primrose path. Lead him to his own destruction.

"Do you believe me?" he asked softly.

She knew he'd do his best to stop it but with a sense of inevitability she knew it was too late. "I don't know what to believe anymore."

"I wish we were still at the lake where that wouldn't matter."

"Me, too," she said quietly, meaning it. If they'd never left she could have continued in the dreamlike state that Scott had evoked in her when they'd been together. He slipped his arm around her waist and pulled her to him. She closed her eyes and held him to her, pretending once again that the con was real. That Scott was real. That she hadn't made a huge mistake by sleeping with him. Because she knew she couldn't sleep with a man just for sex. Scott meant more to her than she'd realized.

Everything crystallized in her mind. Seeing Scott and Stevie talking together had reinforced what she already knew. She couldn't trust him. She couldn't trust gamblers. She couldn't trust Scott Rivers.

But why then did she feel as if he was the other part of her soul? Why then did his arms around her feel like the home she'd never had, the home she'd always searched for? Why then did she, who'd made it her life's goal to be honest and real with herself, want to pretend she'd never heard of his bet?

* * *

Scott held her in his arms and knew that everything was spiraling out of his control. He'd ended the bet with Stevie, telling him that Raine had shot him down for the last time and that Stevie had won. Stevie had ribbed him about losing but said he'd been frozen out by Raine, as well.

When the pictures hit the paper, they would be the end to Raine's career as well.

Scott could understand that she wouldn't want him then. He hoped one day she'd meet a man who could give her what she needed. What he wanted her to have. He already knew that he couldn't be that man.

Still, he couldn't help but try.

He couldn't get her out of his head. After making love to her all day, he'd hated the fact that they'd had to return to Vegas and go back to work. Go back to being with other people. He'd wanted to keep them both naked at the lake house for weeks, maybe months.

He wanted them to spend their days and nights just talking, teasing and making love. He knew his hold on her was fragile.

He'd already called his accountant and made arrangements for the money to be wired to Stevie's bank in the morning. The loss of the money didn't bother him. Now he had to get on the phone with his lawyers and he should do it now, but he had the feeling that if he let Raine go, he'd have a hard time getting her back in his arms.

He just hoped that she didn't know about the bet and that he could confess things before it got worse.

Stevie wasn't the kind of guy that Scott could ask to keep a secret. All in all that wasn't one of his better decisions—taking the bet. He'd only done it because… well, his ego was feeling a little bruised by the way she'd kept ignoring him. Now he felt like an idiot.

He'd cleared the way to confess to Raine. But not tonight. She seemed almost fragile tonight, which didn't fit with the woman he'd come to know.

He didn't know how else to bind her to him except to give her all the things women liked. Picnics, romance, jewelry, chocolate. But were those things enough to keep Raine? She wasn't like other women. She saw the ruse he used to keep everyone at bay.

"I have a surprise for you tomorrow afternoon," he said, rubbing his hands down her back.

She tipped her head back and looked up at him. "What makes you think I'm available?"

"Are you going to be difficult?" he asked, tracing one finger down the side of her neck and along the ribbed edge of her T-shirt.

She nodded. "I don't want to be like all the other women you've known."

"You aren't. You keep me on my toes."

"Someone needs to."

She was sassing him and he liked it. There was something low-spirited about Raine tonight and he couldn't figure out what it was.

"Okay, if you don't want to have the adventure of a lifetime."

"Whose lifetime—yours or mine?"

"Both of ours. It'll be a first for both of us."

"What is it?" she asked.

"A flight in Deacon's helicopter to Hoover Dam."

"Who's Deacon?"

"One of my buddies, remember, the other trouble-maker."

"Oh, that one. You've never flown in a helicopter before?"

"Yes, I have, but not with you. I thought we'd take a picnic with us and have dinner before coming back to the hotel."

He led her away from the stone path and into the maze. The night air was filled with the scent of jasmine—his mother's favorite plant. He kept Raine tucked up under his shoulder as they moved through the maze.

She bit her lower lip and wouldn't really look at him. "I'm tired."

"Tired of me?" he asked. That was his real fear. That by being himself, he'd somehow bored her. He could play a more exciting role, be anything she needed him to be.

She stopped then. "No, Scott. Tired of me. Tired of replaying the same things in my head."

"What things? Maybe I can help."

She shook her head. "I have to do this myself."

"Can I take you upstairs and make you forget about your troubles?"

She turned to him then. The moonlight fell softly over the planes of her face. "Yes. I think I'd like that."

He bent and kissed her. He couldn't get enough of her mouth, and when she looked up at him with her eyes filled with some indefinable emotion, he needed to. He wanted to wipe away the sadness he sensed in her and replace it with…what? He couldn't be responsible for another person's happiness, no matter how much he wanted to be.

He slipped his key card from his pocket. "My suite number is 2435. Go on up. I'll meet you there."

"What are you going to do?"

"Call my lawyers and take care of that picture. Then I'll be up."

"Thanks," she said.

"Honey, I wouldn't do anything to hurt you."

"Really, Scott?"

"I wouldn't lie to you, Raine. I know that we haven't known each other long, but you're too important to me for me to lie."

She stepped away from him. "I'm glad to hear that. I don't think I could ever forgive a man who lied to me."

She walked away from him, and he felt the weight of his actions and his words fall heavily around his shoulders. He knew he was going to have to tell her about Stevie's bet. But he also knew he needed time to bind her to him. And romantic dates weren't going to be enough. He needed to bind her to him first with her body and then hopefully her heart and soul would follow.

Raine let herself into Scott's suite and waited for him. His suite was larger than hers and overlooked the hotel's waterfall and pool. It was made up of two rooms and a small balcony. She walked through the two rooms and steeled herself to continue playing the role she'd selected for herself. The role of a woman falling in love with a man who was too good to be true.

If only it were a role and not the real thing. She knew she was going to have to push aside those doubts. That very real feeling of being betrayed by a man she'd let herself care for. She'd been doing a better job of it before—no, she hadn't. And she refused to lie to herself. She'd been falling in love with Scott since the moment she'd met him.

The room was opulently appointed and though she knew Scott would feel comfortable in this room, she now knew this wasn't the real man. The man she was coming to know was more comfortable in a relaxed setting. She trailed her fingers over the leather love seat in the sitting room before opening the French doors leading to the balcony and stepping outside.

That was the hard part. The glimpses she'd had of the real Scott Rivers all added up to a man who really wouldn't be able to make a bet about getting a woman he cared for into bed.

She wished he'd just confess to her what he'd done. That way she could try to figure out if he was sincere in his pursuit of her—which, her heart told her, he had to be—or whether he'd just been playing one of those kinky games that bored, wealthy men sometimes played.

He was out of her league on so many levels. But

were they only surface things, as she wanted to believe, or were they things that went bone deep?

She curled her fingers around the cold wrought-iron bars that lined the balcony and stared blindly down at the fantasy world of the Chimera. A world designed to entice its visitors to forget about the mundane details of everyday life and indulge themselves in their fantasies. To forget the consequences of their everyday world and just live for the moment.

She heard the suite door open but stayed where she was on the balcony. She didn't want to face Scott yet.

She heard his footfalls on the carpeted floor as he came toward her. He paused on the landing just before stepping out on the balcony, where she was.

"My lawyers are taking care of the pictures. I think we got to it in time."

She didn't turn around and look at him. She needed to pretend that this was real. That here in the land of the ultimate illusion they'd found something to believe in.

"Honey?"

She didn't want to talk. She wanted to lose herself in his arms once more. To feed the fantasy that was so believable until they'd returned here.

"Make love to me out here."

He stepped out onto the balcony, his arms closing around her from behind. His hands skimmed down her body, lingering to cup her breasts and to tease her nipples through the layers of her T-shirt and bra. She laid her head back on his shoulder, turned her head so she could kiss his neck.

He lifted her shirt, pushed her bra out of the way and cupped her breasts. He held them up, and she noticed him staring down at her exposed body. Her nipples were beaded and hard from the combination of his touch and the cold night air. She shivered and undulated against him.

He plucked at her nipples until she moaned his name. She needed him. Turning in his embrace, she leaned up on her toes and kissed him. She thrust her tongue deep in his mouth and rubbed her aroused breasts against his chest.

She wedged her hands between them and ripped open his shirt. The buttons fell to the floor and she pushed the shirt off his shoulders. She needed him now. She wanted to feel his warm, naked skin on hers.

She rubbed her breasts against his chest and heard him moan. She felt his hands skimming down her back and cupping her butt, pulling her more fully against his erection.

She adjusted her body against him so that he was rubbing right where she needed him to be. He lifted her up and suckled her nipple, biting lightly at her flesh and then soothing it with his tongue. She wrapped her legs around his hips and rocked against him.

He suckled her other nipple into his mouth, pulling so strongly at her that she felt her womb clench. She wanted him inside her now.

She slid off his body, undoing her jeans and pushing them down her legs. "I need you now."

"Me, too, honey."

He turned her around, put her hands on the wrought-iron railing. "Don't let go."

She couldn't have if her life depended on it. She felt his mouth at the nape of her neck then the scraping of his teeth down the line of her spine. Then he returned to her nape and traced his tongue down her back.

She shivered with each touch of his mouth on her skin. Her entire body was extremely sensitized, and she felt as if she was going to peak at any moment but held off the inevitable because the waiting felt so good. And she wanted him deep inside her when she had her orgasm.

His fingers traced the crease in her buttocks, then she felt the nip of his teeth on each cheek. "You have such a nice ass, honey."

She bit her lip as his fingers dipped lower, found her wet and ready for him. As always his fingers were firm, his caresses arousing her so much that in a meeting she'd seen him shake hands with Hayden and had immediately felt his fingers on her skin.

The way he rubbed his hand over her belly just before he entered her. The way he caught her wrists in one hand while he thrust into her. The way his callused hands aroused her to the point of no return.

Then he was pressed against her back. His jeans felt rough against her, his erection prodded at the small of her back. She reached between their bodies, caressing him and freeing him from the confines of his jeans. She was surprised to feel him naked under his pants.

He thrust into her palm and she cupped him, held

him while he moved against her. "I wanted to be ready for you this time."

"Condom?"

"One minute."

She heard him opening the packet and glanced over her shoulder to watch him put it on.

"Open your legs a little wider."

She did and he bent his knees and entered her from behind. He held himself just inside her until she squirmed and pushed herself back on him. He slid all the way home and she felt her body quiver. She knew it wasn't going to take more than a thrust to push her over the edge. He slid his hand down her body, his fingers finding that little bud between her legs.

"Come for me, Raine," he said, circling it with his finger as he started thrusting deep inside her.

She did and then again before he finally found his release inside her. He held her carefully in his arms, both of them spent. He separated their bodies and carried her inside, making love to her again in his bed.

Ten

The next few weeks Scott dedicated himself to keeping Raine happy. The *Enquirer* had caught three more photos of him, but he'd been careful to stay away from Raine in public. He didn't like it, but he'd had to sneak into her room, or her into his, late at night. He'd won his week of matches and now had one more week of shooting with the three champions from the other weeks.

Raine had been in Vegas the entire time and he stayed in the background during her time on the set. He flew his parents in to meet her and they'd spent the weekend at his lake house. Raine had gone there with Kylie and Shelby to visit and then later Deacon and Hayden had arrived so that there was no way a picture of just Raine and him could be taken.

His mom adored Raine and told him if he let her get away, she'd never forgive him. Scott needed some solid advice, and his dad was the kind who would be able to help him out. But in the end Scott, who'd always been the good son, couldn't tell them that he'd made a bet about Raine and ask for some suggestions on how to break that news to her.

But tonight that would end; tonight he planned to tell her everything at dinner. Hayden was waiting for him in the lobby of the Chimera. He liked his friend but didn't really want to see him right now.

"There's a major problem," Hayden said.

"What do you mean?"

"We've got a pack of paparazzi waiting outside that door for you and Raine."

"Both of us, why?"

"Gossip on the set was leaked to the press and the *Enquirer* ran that picture you suppressed a few weeks ago. Then one of the players speculated you've been sleeping with Raine to continue being on the show. And Steve let slip you bet him 50K you'd get her into bed."

"What's it like out there?"

"Crazy. Sal is running interference and I've called Deacon and few of the other hotel owners to see if there is anyone bigger in town who can take the heat off of you two."

"Any luck?"

"No. They latched on to your story because it's a slow news week."

Scott wanted to put his hand through a wall. He'd

waited too long to come clean with Raine, and now it was going to be too little, too late. This was why he'd stuck to relationships built on movie screens or television sets. He sucked at real life.

"What the hell were you thinking?" Hayden asked him. "You know Stevie can't keep his mouth shut."

"I wasn't thinking. I knew I wanted Raine and nothing would stop me from having her…so betting on it didn't seem a bad thing."

Hayden clapped his hand on Scott's shoulder, and though no words were spoken he knew his friend would do whatever he could to help him. He swallowed hard.

"I managed to catch Raine before she walked into the lobby."

"Where is she?"

"In my office. I've got the monitors on so we can keep an eye on the paparazzi."

When they reached his office, Hayden pushed open the door, but Scott didn't enter. Raine sat huddled, sipping some kind of hot beverage. He'd never seen her look so small or fragile as she did in that moment. He started to really hate himself when he saw her. He knew that he'd convinced her to play for high stakes. And she'd lost.

He'd never allowed himself to think there would be anything but a happy ending for them. After all, it was what he was used to. But now he was standing a short distance from the press who all wanted to take photos of a woman he'd bet fifty thousand dollars that he could take to bed.

Shelby was there with her but still Raine kept to

herself. Scott didn't know what to do. He'd always been the press's darling. He liked them; they liked him. He'd never done anything that would sell papers like this story would.

Joel was en route. They both knew that Raine would be losing her job and there was a fairly good chance Scott wouldn't be playing in the championship this week. He didn't give a crap about that.

What pissed him off was that he'd ever made the bet. A big part of him acknowledged it was because he was so used to winning, so used to getting his own way, that it had ticked him off when she'd kept turning him down.

"Can we have a moment, Hayden?" Scott asked. He just wanted to make this right.

"Um, I'm not sure how to say this, but this is the wrong time for you to be alone with your woman."

He knew Hayden was right. But he didn't care. This was what happened when he tried to be himself. When he stopped playing the roles he knew how to play. And he had to fix it.

"Will you get the press assembled in a room? Tell them I'll release a statement."

Hayden made a few calls and put the entire thing in motion. Raine still hadn't glanced up at him or said a word to him. Shelby, Hayden's sweet wife, was also there, glaring daggers at him.

"I'm not leaving," she said.

Scott barely nodded at her. Raine still wouldn't look at him, and he knew he needed to do some fast thinking if he wanted to make this right. He stepped back out of Hayden's office and called his folks. His dad was still up watching the late news.

"I need you and Mom to come to Vegas tonight."

"What's the matter?"

"I screwed up, Dad. Big time. And I hurt Raine. She…doesn't have the kind of family we do, so will you and Mom come here?"

"Tell me what happened," his father said.

Scott did. Not sparing himself or Raine in the telling, he just explained his stupid bet. And then ended with the paparazzi camped in Hayden's hotel.

"Get her out of there. We'll meet her at the lake house."

"Take my plane, Dad. I've got them readying it."

They hung up a few minutes later, and Scott was aware that his parents were disappointed in him. It was the first time he'd had to call them to bail him out of something stupid he'd done, and he didn't like it. He liked being the golden boy. He liked the kind of life he had when he was golden and not some kind of schmuck. He'd wager that Raine was thinking the same thing.

Deacon pushed through the door at the end of the hallway. "Hayden called me. Kylie's out front with the Mercedes and she's volunteered to get Raine out of here."

"Thanks, Deacon. She's pretty mad at me—"

"Say no more. I'll go talk to her. Hayden's got them distracted. I'll take care of your woman."

Scott's heart skipped a beat. If only she were still his woman. But he had a feeling when he sorted this mess out, she was never going to talk to him again.

Joel walked in a few minutes later, and a bold photographer pushed his way past Hayden's security guards to snap pictures of Scott in the hallway. The guards grabbed him and forced him back into the casino.

"This is a hell of a mess, Rivers. I'll need to see Raine privately, then you. Don't go anywhere."

"I'm not leaving."

Joel had left her alone after terminating her contract. He wouldn't bring legal action, because as he said, the ways of the heart didn't give a damn about legal obligations. His words echoed in her mind as she sat in the passenger seat of Kylie Prescott's Mercedes, riding through the night toward Scott's lake house. Shelby sat in the backseat.

Raine felt a certain sense of comfort from the other women. They were both so indignant on her behalf and upset with Scott. She felt almost guilty about it. They didn't know that she'd run her own con. That she'd played Scott and herself in a dangerous game involving both of their hearts. Now she was jobless and she had no one to blame but herself.

"I know how you feel," Kylie said into the quiet.

"I doubt that," Raine said. She honestly didn't think any other person understood how she felt. They couldn't possibly unless they'd had a glimpse of the kind of life they'd always longed for. One filled not only with a job they loved, but with the kind of man who she'd never imagined could exist.

"You're angry, hurt, you can't believe that you could fall for a man who'd think making a bet about you was a good idea."

She glanced at Kylie. "That sounds like the voice of experience."

"It is. Hayden bet Deacon he couldn't convince me to marry him. I didn't find out until after we were married." Kylie shook her head at the memories. "Deacon had some idea about marrying the perfect woman."

Raine studied the woman. Kylie was pretty and obviously in love with her husband. And she was kind. Nice and quiet in a bookish sort of way with her horn-rim glasses and her conservative clothing. It was hard to think she was the ideal woman for a gambler like Deacon.

"Scott wasn't looking for the perfect woman. He was looking to prove he could thaw my ice-queen image."

She felt a little raw when she thought about it. What he'd thought of her and how he'd acted.

"Who'd he bet with?" Shelby asked from the backseat. "I know Hayden and Deacon both learned their lesson from what happened with Kylie. And I don't think Max would bet on a woman."

"Stevie Taylor."

"Scott should have known better. Stevie spends more time on the cover of the tabloids than he does onstage."

Raine said nothing. She couldn't fully blame Scott, because she'd known about the bet and could have walked away. She should have, but there'd been something about him that enticed her. "I knew about the bet. I conned Scott into falling for me so I could push him away."

Kylie took her eyes from the road, her face illuminated in the dashboard lights. Raine felt like her father's daughter in that moment. She wondered how he ever got used to that feeling that came from knowing you'd used someone for your own good.

"But you fell for him, didn't you?" Shelby asked.

Raine had never had any girlfriends and wasn't sure she liked talking about her feelings, but there was something so easy about these women. "Yes, I guess I did."

"To be honest, these guys are good men, they just make error judgments. With Deacon it's because he grew up without any parental supervision. He learned to scheme and con to get everything he wanted. It never occurred to him not to wager on me."

Raine leaned deeper in the seat. Scott didn't have that excuse. "I think Scott is so used to playing roles that he doesn't always think about the consequences until after he gets into the part he's playing."

But Scott had soon stopped acting around her. She wished she'd met him at a different time. Like now, when she had no job and lots of time on her hands.

They arrived at the lake house. Kylie handed her the key that she'd gotten from Scott before they'd left the Chimera. "You don't have to stay," Raine said.

"Yes, we do. You might want to talk."

"I'm really not that type of person."

"Well, if you change your mind we'll be here," Shelby said firmly.

Raine opened the door and they turned on the lights as they entered the house. Raine felt Scott's absence keenly.

Shelby came to stand next to her. "Listen, Raine," she said softly, "I also have been where you are—"

"I don't think so." Shelby owned a very successful chain of lingerie stores, Bêcheur d'Or, so Raine highly doubted that the sophisticated woman standing next to her really had ever been where she was.

"I married Hayden for his money," Shelby said bluntly.

"What?"

"I took a million dollars from his dad to leave him at the altar when we were both too young to be married. So believe me when I say I know what you're feeling."

Shelby explained how she'd come back to Vegas to make up for her past with Hayden and ended up falling for him again. Only this time they both were honest with each other.

Raine stared at her. Maybe these two women did understand her. "I can't forgive myself for trying to fool him like that. I mean, I know he didn't start out with the best intentions, but I still shouldn't have played him like I did."

The other women watched her for a minute and then gave her a hug. For the first time ever, Raine felt it was okay that she was flawed. These women weren't perfect and their husbands hadn't always done the right thing, but they'd made their relationships work. So maybe there might be hope for her and Scott.

Later that night as she lay in Scott's bed, she replayed the day in her head and realized that she now had a clean slate. A chance to go to Scott as a woman in the open, not lying to him, not hiding from him and not hiding from herself.

His parents had gone up to the lake house, and Shelby and Kylie had returned to town. Scott had avoided them, not really wanting to know that there was no hope left for him and Raine. So instead he'd made a public apology on every entertainment news program who'd have him on. He took out ads in *Variety, Premiere, Entertainment Weekly* and *USA Today* apologizing formally for his crass bet. Stevie had done the same thing at Scott's insistence.

It turned out Stevie had made an offhand comment about the bet to one of his bandmates and this had been overheard by a tabloid journalist who'd been in town to cover Paris Hilton's latest party.

Scott knew that Raine had been used in her life by her father and her brother. He also knew that the one thing she'd always counted on—her job—had been taken from her because of him. He'd hurt her on so many levels that getting her back was going to involve more than just candy and flowers.

He racked his brain for something that would

convince her that he wasn't a schmuck and that she should take him back. Finally he figured out what he had to do.

He approached Joel and since Joel had been rooting for them from the beginning, he agreed to do something a little unorthodox. It took a lot of planning and finessing but at last every detail was in place.

He had Joel call her back to Vegas to say he had a few questions for her about the show. Then he waited until she was back in the hotel. Hayden had offered him the use of the penthouse garden-side balcony and Scott took him up on it.

He was going to ask Raine to be his wife. He was going to come clean with her, then apologize and make love to her.

He held the bouquet of stargazer lilies in one hand and a small bag from Bêcheur d'Or in the other and waited in a private lounge for the elevator to arrive. He'd sent the invitation for dinner to her room. He had no idea if she'd show up, but Hayden and Deacon had both promised to watch the monitors for her.

His cell phone rang. "Rivers."

"It's Hayden. She's on her way."

"Thanks," he said, then hung up.

The elevator opened and she stood there looking up at him wearily. "What are you doing here?"

"Coming clean." He handed her the flowers. "Have dinner with me tonight."

Scott had ordered Italian food because he knew that Raine loved it. And she'd been eating from craft services for the last few weeks. Between Hayden and Deacon they had the most accomplished chefs in Nevada on staff. He'd asked for dishes he knew would keep well. He hadn't wanted servers or anyone else in this paradise he'd created.

He'd studied for this role carefully. In his experience every woman wanted a man with a three-part combination that included the suaveness and sexiness of James Bond, the intelligence and wit of Robert Redford in *Legal Eagles* and the safety and security of Michael Keaton in *Mr. Mom.*

He led them to a satin-draped table where candlelight sparkled off two Waterford flutes. He pulled out her chair, and before he sat he poured them both a glass of champagne and took a deep breath. Now that the moment was here he couldn't remember any of the performances he'd studied. He nervously felt under his chair for the ring box. It was exactly where he'd secured it with gaffers' tape earlier.

He snapped it open and felt the diamond ring waiting there. It was his great-grandmother's ring. An antique platinum setting. His father had been happy to give it to Scott, ready for his son to settle down and very happy with the woman he'd selected.

Now if only she'd have him. Scott knew there was a big chance she'd say no. Raine didn't make snap decisions. And she wasn't one to do anything without weighing the consequences.

He finally found his voice. "First I want to apologize for not making sure those photographers stayed away from you. And for not taking the threat to your job as seriously as I should have."

"You weren't the only one to blame," she said carefully, but she wouldn't look at him and that hurt. Had he killed every bit of feeling she'd had for him?

He cleared his throat and lifted his champagne flute. She lifted hers as well.

They both took a sip. She moved to set her glass down, and Scott realized the time was at hand. He needed to…just do it.

He pushed to his feet, startling her and bumping the table. He shoved the ring into his pocket and tried to recall the smooth moves he'd studied to get ready for this night.

His mind drew a blank.

"Scott?"

He came around the table to her side, then leaned one hip on the edge of the table, facing her. His hands were sweating. Dammit, he never sweated. Not even when he'd debuted on Broadway at the age of twelve.

He wiped his palms on his pants. "I have something…to say. Those weeks we spent together were the best of my life. I've always had a rich life, I'm not denying that, but you've added a new dimension. One I didn't realize was missing until you stepped onto the set and gave me direction. And I know that I screwed up majorly, but I hope that this will help make up for it."

She tipped her face back to look up at him. In his mind's eye he saw her the way he wanted her—her lips swollen from his kisses, her eyes soft and wide, her skin still a little flushed—and he wanted her again.

He wanted to say the hell with all these trappings of romance and take her back to his suite. He wanted to lay her in the center of his bed and make love to her, and when she was limp with exhaustion from his loving, he wanted to slip the ring on her finger and make her his forever.

"Are you okay?" she asked.

He realized he was standing over her just staring at her. "Yes. I'm trying to tell you that you gave me something I've never found with anyone else. With you I don't have to be 'on' all the time. With you I have the luxury of being myself and I'm finding I actually like it."

"You might believe that I gave you that but it was already there. You're a very generous man and a loyal friend. I had nothing to do with that." Her words weren't reluctant and he saw she was sincere.

"Yes, you did. You made me comfortable in my own skin. Made me want to be better than I've ever been before."

"Well, you've done the same for me. I think I would have continued on, carefully keeping all men at arm's length for the rest of my life, if you hadn't pushed your way closer."

"You were just waiting for the right Prince Charming."

"Now you're an animated character. Really, Scott, is there no end to your talents?"

"What can I say? You lucked out when you met me," he said.

"And hardly any ego."

"You're right. I should have said I lucked out when I met you. I really did, Raine. My life…well, let's just say you've given me purpose."

She bit her lip. "I swear if you say I complete you, I'm not going to be responsible for my actions."

"Dammit, woman. I'm trying to tell you something important."

"Then stop trying to be whatever you think I want. Just lay it on the line. Why am I here? So you can make amends before you jet off to your next exciting locale?"

He dropped to one knee in front of her. "No, honey. Never. What I'm trying to tell you is that…"

He couldn't say the words out loud. He realized now that he always just said "Me, too," when his mom said them to him. Always just settled for a gruff hug with the old man when it came time to say goodbye.

"What?"

And here was Raine. A woman who needed the words from him. As he looked up at her, he knew he needed to say them. To make this moment as real as it could be. To know that this wasn't just another memory he thought he had that turned out to be a scene from a play or a TV show.

"I love you," he said.

Her eyes went wide and jaw dropped. "Scott, I don't know what to—"

"I'm not done yet. I want you to marry me."

She swallowed as he pulled the ring from his pocket and held it up to her. "This was my great-grandmother's ring. It was one of the only possessions she brought with her from Italy when she came to the U.S." He slid it on her finger. "It would give me a great feeling of honor and pride if you'd say you'll marry me and wear this ring."

Eleven

Raine looked down at the antique ring on her finger, unable to believe what she'd heard. What he'd asked her. She wanted to say yes. She wanted to somehow find a way to make what they'd shared real enough that they both could spend the rest of their days together.

"Raine?" he asked, still on his knee in front of her.

His hand felt big and warm around hers. Safe in a way that she wanted to be for the rest of her life. But he was more than safety. He was more than she'd expected, and she knew that she'd been falling for him. "I…I don't know if I can."

"Why not?" he asked, pushing to his feet.

She tipped her head back to look up at him. Marriage was unexpected, though she'd had an inkling he'd been thinking of long-term with her when he'd brought her to meet his parents.

It had been obvious from that weekend where the "real" Scott came from. His parents were retired teachers who had a strong sense of self and community. To be honest they were the kind of parents she'd always craved for herself. And Scott was the kind of man she'd dreamed of having by her side, except for his penchant for adventure and gaming.

"I haven't been thinking of us in those kinds of terms."

He went back to his seat, reached across the table and took her hands in his. "How can you not be? I know that feelings this strong can't be one-sided."

Tears burned the back of her eyes. "You're right, but how do we both know that it's not just this wonderful setting?"

"Hell, I'd feel the same if we were in your hotel room or at Red Rock or riding on the Harley. It's you, Raine. You're the one I want to spend my days and nights with. The one I want to hold in my arms and make love to every chance we get. The one I need by my side."

His words moved her. She saw the truth in them and it scared her. She did love Scott. There was no doubt inside her that she loved him. But was it real? She was so afraid to believe it.

They'd both spent their entire relationship in Vegas not living real lives. They'd also both spent the entire time lying to each other, and she was the one who knew it. "Honey, I swear you won't regret it."

"It's not that I fear I'll regret it."

"What are you afraid of?"

"That this isn't real. You're a gambler not only by luck and skill but by design. Everything in your life is a risk or a challenge or a dare."

He shook his head.

"Our first date was a dare. That's how you approach life and how you live it. I'm not like that. I have dreams about marriage, Scott. Dreams of what I think a husband and wife should be."

"I can make them come true," he said. "You say that I live for a dare or a challenge. Tell me what you want and I'll make that my challenge, wrapping you in my love and keeping you happy all the rest of our days."

How could she say no? How could she not reach out and take what he was offering her? He offered her the fulfillment of the secret dreams she'd always held.

"Let's make our dreams come true," he said.

And she flashed back to her father saying the same words to her so many times throughout her youth. She knew that Scott wasn't her dad. Knew he had money… now.

"Dreams aren't what life is about," she said, slipping the ring from her finger.

"What are you talking about?"

"I'm not the right woman for you. You need someone who is willing to play your games, someone who is happy living from moment to moment. And I'm not that woman."

"You could be," he said, taking the ring and holding it in his hand. He took her wrist with his other hand, brushing a kiss against the center of her palm. "And I could be the perfect man for you."

She closed her eyes against the truth she saw in his. This was what her life was going to come down to. This one moment when she either had to take a chance on Scott—take a chance on falling for her own con and knowing for the rest of her days that she had tricked him into loving her—or walk away and spend the rest of her days alone.

"I'm so afraid that this won't translate away from Vegas. That once you see me in the real world, you'll realize all the reasons you don't want me as your wife."

He shook his head, kissing her palm one more time and then her wrist. He placed the ring in the center of her palm and closed her fingers gently over it. "I could never do that, honey."

"You say that now when things are going well. You've been winning on the show and at the tables here in Vegas. But what if your winning streak ends? Then what will happen?"

He said nothing and she knew he couldn't. She was bringing him down and hadn't intended that. She should have ended things a long time ago, before either of them had to be hurt. And she knew Scott was hurting, as well. But she couldn't marry him. She just couldn't.

She opened her hand, stared at this family heirloom that he'd been willing to give to her. "I'm sorry, Scott, but I can't marry you."

She handed him back the ring and walked away from the magic of the night, the magic of the man, the magic of love. Because Raine Montgomery knew that magic was just an illusion.

Scott watched her walk away, unable to believe that this night was going so wrong. He pocketed the ring and ran to her, stopping her before she could get on the elevator.

"You can't just walk away."

"Yes, I can." There were tracks from her tears running down her face, and it was like taking a body blow to the gut.

He pulled her into his arms, not wanting to see her hurt. He hadn't meant to hurt her with this. He wanted to resolve their affair. To make it more than a temporary thing. Having fallen in love for the first time, he wanted to show her to the world.

She sniffed and he found his handkerchief in his back pocket and handed it to her. She wiped her eyes.

"Thank you." She neatly refolded the handkerchief and handed it back to him.

"There's no reason for this, Raine. We can have a long engagement if you need time to come to terms with marrying me."

"It's not just that." She took a few steps back, putting some distance between them, wrapping her arms around her waist.

"Then what the hell is it?" he asked, frustrated that he couldn't get her to see what their lives could be, that she wasn't buying into his vision of their future together. She was standing in the exact same spot she'd been in earlier, when everything had been going smoothly. Earlier, before his carefully rehearsed evening had gone to hell.

"I…can't trust you," she said, biting her lower lip.

"You did before the press showed up and ruined everything."

"I mean with my heart," she said quietly.

"Dammit, I'm not your father, Raine. I'm not going to make promises, get your eyes shining in anticipation and then never deliver. Don't you know that by now?" he asked. He knew this romance thing would backfire. If he had her in bed…but they couldn't spend their lives together in bed. Sex obviously wasn't a problem between them. What had he missed?

She shook her head and he realized that being the kind and caring suitor wasn't getting the job done. "Don't make me pay for your father's sins."

"Is that what you think this is about? Some payback for all the times any man has wronged me?"

He shrugged. He had no idea what was going through her mind right now. "It seems to me that you are still running. I'm not going to dare you to marry me. This is too important to me. You are too important to me.

"You need to take a leap of faith and trust that I'll be here to catch you. But until you're ready to do that, we don't have anything." He held his arms open, inviting her back into his embrace.

"Trust works both ways, right?" she asked, not moving.

He dropped his arms to his sides. "Of course it does."

"How does lying fit into the entire trust scheme?" she asked in a silky tone that made the hairs on the back of his neck rise.

"What are you talking about? I'm not lying to you."

"You already have done that, Scott." She dropped her arms to her sides and took a step forward, no longer vulnerable but angry.

"When?" he asked, afraid she was referring to the bet.

"When you made a bet about getting me in bed and then seduced me by being the man of my dreams."

He didn't attempt to deny it. "I'm trying to make it right by asking you to marry me."

"Don't try to explain. I might start to believe in this fairy tale you've created."

"How did you hear about it?"

"I overheard you that first day."

"Why didn't you say something that day in the booth?"

"Why didn't you?" she countered. "I was so angry with you. Believe it or not I'd started to weaken and was thinking about maybe going out with you after filming was over."

"But then, like an ass, I made that bet," he said. Having come to know Raine and fallen in love with her, he realized that he'd done something she'd never be able to forgive. He'd known that for a while now but had thought he could tell her about it after they were a couple, when he could convince her to forgive him.

"Exactly," she said. "And I got angry."

"What do you mean?" He didn't know the woman standing before him now. The softness and the caring he'd come to associate with Raine were gone. Her eyes, which usually broadcast whatever she felt, were cold.

"I mean you really pissed me off. And I decided to see if I still had it."

"Had what?"

She walked right up to him, ran her fingers across the stubble on his jaw. "The ability to run a con."

"What kind of con?" he asked, because he needed to know how deeply they'd both played each other and themselves.

"The perfect con, the one to make Mr. Charming fall in love with me."

"Are you trying to tell me this has all been an act?"

She nodded.

"I don't buy it. You might have started out planning to make me fall for you, like a first-class grifter, but it changed, didn't it? You fell for your own con."

"There were times I was tempted, but then I'd remember—this is a man who's got a lot of money riding on making me fall for him, and that's not something I can love."

This time she walked away and he let her go.

Raine was shaking as she entered the elevator car. Everything had gone horribly wrong. She felt ashamed of herself for what she'd done to Scott. It didn't matter that he'd been lying to her. All that really mattered was that she wanted to get away.

She'd lost Scott and a little of her self-respect in the process. She wrapped her arms around her own waist and leaned against the back door of the elevator car. When the door opened, she tried to wipe her tears. She was surprised to see Scott standing there.

She realized she'd never selected a floor, so the car had stayed where it was.

"Oh, honey, come here."

She shook her head, but he came to her and pulled her into his arms. She couldn't hold back her tears, and she fought not to sob out loud at how right he felt wrapped around her. A part of her wanted to say to hell with cons and bets and just start over.

But trust wasn't easily won from either of them. He stroked his hands up and down her back, and she just clung to him, hiding in his strength one last time.

"I ended the bet with Stevie, told him he won and paid him the money. I don't want you to think that I would sleep with you for the money."

"If you did you overpaid," she said, because she wanted to hurt him, maybe even wanted to hurt them both. This wasn't easy. She didn't think it ever would be. A part of her wished she'd never told him she knew, so then she could have continued the ruse forever.

"Don't do that. You are so sensual, willing to do whatever I ask of you. I swear, woman, I'll never get enough of you in my bed."

She felt the same way. Scott had unlocked a hidden part of her soul that she'd never thought really mattered. Sex had always been something she did when she needed to feel close to another human being. When she needed to be held, she'd date a guy a few times, have sex with him and then move on.

But she couldn't move on now. She knew it. Scott had changed something inside her, and while she might have been trying to con him into falling for her, she knew she was the one who'd been conned. Conned into forgetting about the circumstances of her actions.

"Come back and let's finish our champagne," he said, taking her by the hand.

She allowed him to lead her back to the table. She followed closely on his heels and took her seat. She sipped the champagne, but the magic of the night was lost in the reality of what they both were.

She wondered if Joel would want to make a reality show based on gamblers and con artists and how if they both mixed it would be to their detriment.

"What are you thinking?" he asked. There was an edge to his voice that had never been there before.

"That we can never trust each other. Aren't you thinking the same thing?" she asked. She knew it had to be true. They'd both been playing with each other. Was their love a by-product of the games or was it the real thing? To be honest that was what scared her—that she'd think it was the real thing and wake up one morning to the truth.

He put his flute down. "I'm trying not to. Just let it go, Raine."

"Don't want to marry me anymore, do you?"

"I didn't say that. But I do realize we don't know each other as well as I thought we did."

"Or maybe we know each other too well. Maybe the fact that you fell for a woman who was acting is too eerie for you."

"I don't think you know what you're talking about."

"Actually, I think I've finally figured it out. We're both actors. I'm pretending that my life can be normal, and you're pretending that your life's not one big play written by someone else's standards."

"If you want to be down on yourself, that's one thing. But I was raised by real people, not someone who taught his daughter to prey on men's emotions for her own gain."

His words hurt, cutting deep into the very heart of her. Part of her knew he was right, but that didn't stop her from getting mad.

"Yeah, your parents must be really proud that you bet on getting a girl in bed."

"What bothers you, Raine? That I made the bet with Stevie or that we both know I won it?"

She pushed to her feet. Gone was the emotional fragility she'd felt earlier. Now she was just angry. Angry enough not to care that she might regret this later. How could she ever have felt she was in love with him?

He was a gambler, a daredevil. All the things she knew better than to fall for.

"I'm sorry, Raine," he said, catching her in his arms before she could leave. "If you're not ready to be my wife, that's okay. I'll wait. But know that I'm ready to be your man."

"I need some time."

He nodded, but he knew time was the last thing she needed. She needed to realize that she trusted him and that he was worthy of that trust.

"No, you don't. You need your man to take control."

Twelve

"How do you plan to do that?" she asked.

His smile was bold and wicked. And he kissed her with all the passion and emotion she'd been afraid to believe he felt for her.

"I'm going to have to blindfold you so you will focus only on me."

She arched one eyebrow at him. "Okay."

From his pocket he took a long, smooth piece of silk he'd gotten from Bêcheur d'Or here in the Chimera. "How do you feel about fur-lined handcuffs?"

"On you?"

"Pink's not really my color. But if you wear them for me, I'll wear them for you."

"That's what I like about you, Scott," she said as he

fastened the blindfold over her eyes, carefully freeing a few strands of her hair.

"What do you like?" he asked.

Her breathing was a bit more rapid. Her skin had a healthy glow to it, and her lips were parted. He leaned forward and stroked his tongue over them, dipping inside to taste her mouth. He was addicted to her mouth. He could spend all night kissing her.

When he pulled back she licked her lips, as if wanting to hold on to the taste of him.

"What do you like about me, honey?" he asked again.

She shook her head. "The fact that you're into kinky things but always play fair."

"Play fair?"

"Yes. I think of it as equal-opportunity bondage."

He threw his head back and laughed. This was going to be the best night of his life. If he had any doubts about asking Raine to spend forever with him, they quickly disappeared. She was everything he wanted in a woman.

He led her to the elevator and put the key card in for the penthouse floor. When the car stopped and the door opened, he bypassed Hayden's apartment and opened the door to the balcony overlooking the garden some fifty floors below. Everything was as he'd planned. Twinkle lights sparkled in the trees, and a table was set with fine china. He bent his head, kissing Raine one more time.

Raine leaned up into Scott's embrace. She loved the feel of his arms around her. He made her forget the worries of her day, forget the emotional doubts that plagued her when they were apart. Like a junkie with her favorite drug, she needed the sweet bliss that being in his arms gave her.

She slid her arms around his waist, then lower, cupping his butt as she canted her own hips toward his.

She pulled her head back, wishing he'd removed the blindfold so she could see where they were. She strained her ears and heard nothing but a light wind and soft music.

His thumb stroked over the pulse at her wrist. His scent surrounded her, and she tipped her head to the side, waiting to see what he had planned for her.

She felt him move around behind her, his breath hot on the nape of her neck. She'd struggled with her hair and finally gotten it up in a fairly decent chignon. His mouth at the base of her neck banished all thoughts of her hair.

He sucked on her skin there. Shivers radiated down her shoulders and arms, spreading over her breasts and down her body. He scraped his teeth along the edges of her bare shoulders.

"Do you like that?" he asked, brushing his lips over her ear.

"Yes."

"You'll like what I have planned next even more."

She felt something smooth run along the neckline of her dress. It was soft, like his mouth on her skin, but cool. A faint flowery scent teased her senses, and she realized it was a rose. He traced the lines of her face with the flower, teasingly drawing it around the edges of the blindfold.

He trailed it down her neck and down the edge of the bodice of her dress. He skimmed it over her arms and then brought it back again to her neck.

"Untie the fastening at the back of your neck."

She hesitated. He kissed her again, this time fiercely, showering her with his masculine skill and power.

"Do it for both of us," he urged.

She lifted her hands and loosened the knot that held the halter dress up. As soon as it was untied, she lowered her arms. The zipper at the side of the dress ensured that the top stayed up.

Scott lowered the front of her dress until she felt the air on her naked breasts. Then the heat of his breath as he traced random patterns over her entire chest with his tongue. She stood there in her heels, blindfold on, breasts exposed, quaking and wanting him.

Then she felt the petal softness of the rose over her skin. With his tongue he followed the same pattern, completely devastating her with the thoroughness of his touch. Her nipples were hard, tight, begging for his attention.

She felt the rose swirl over first one nipple then the other. He repeated his caresses between her two nipples until she was ready to scream. She reached up and grabbed for his wrist, catching only two of his fingers.

"Enough, Scott. I can't take any more."

Her breasts were so sensitive she felt like one more brush of that rose and she'd lose it. He twisted his fingers in hers, capturing her wrist and bringing it around to the small of her back. She felt him fasten a bracelet of some sort to her wrist. It was soft, like some kind of fur. A second later her other wrist was surrounded by an identical bracelet. "Am I wearing the handcuffs?"

"Yes. Are you comfortable?" he asked, his concern genuine.

She laughed out loud. She was standing outside with her breasts bare, her wrists behind her back in furry pink handcuffs and wearing a blindfold and, honestly, she'd never felt safer.

"I'll take that as a yes."

"I thought we were going to have dinner."

"In a little while. I'm still working on broadening your horizons beyond the missionary position."

Scott had made love to her two or three times a night when they'd slept together, which was nearly every single night since the first time. He always pushed her sexual boundaries further than she'd have felt comfortable with any other man.

That was what scared her the most about Scott. He wasn't content in just knowing her surface personality. The Raine everyone else thought they knew. He liked to push past those barriers and find…her heart.

"Are you excited?" he asked.

"What do you think?" She didn't like to make things easy for him.

She felt her skirt rise and then his hand on the left cheek of her buttocks. She was wearing a thong, and he traced the back of it down between her legs. "Ah, I'd say yes."

He tugged the fabric to the side, circling his finger

around her pouting flesh. Her legs trembled and she swayed, and he put an arm around her waist, holding her up as his finger entered her.

He continued to touch her intimately until she hung on to her sanity by only a thread. Then she felt the heat of his mouth on her nipple, biting lightly.

"Scott."

"Hmm," he murmured against her skin. He suckled her deeply in time to the thrusting of his fingers inside her. Colors danced behind her eyelids as everything in her body clenched and her climax washed over her. She dug her fingernails into her palms.

He kept his touch between her legs until her body stopped clenching. He kissed her gently on the lips, then refastened her bodice, removed the handcuffs and her blindfold.

She stared at him with a dazed look on her face. His erection pushed against the front of his dress pants but he led her to a round table set on a bed of rose petals and lit by twinkling lights strung in potted trees.

"That's just the beginning of the surprises I have in store for you tonight."

She swallowed against the love she felt rising up in her for this man. Feelings that threatened the belief she'd always held about men, and made it a lie.

"You trust me, baby. You trust me with your body and your heart. Sooner or later you're going to say the words."

After they ate, he lifted her in his arms and carried her around the corner of the balcony to the tent that he'd had set up and the bed of silk pillows he'd made inside. He'd borrowed it from one of the sheiks who frequented the casino. Ali liked to take the tent out into the desert for a week after gambling.

Scott wanted this night to be romance and fairy tales…all the dreams that Raine had ever dreamed made true by him.

He'd saved the hardest task for last. Not that convincing the woman he loved to forgive him was a task, but it was the hardest thing he'd ever done. He'd read books, watched movies, asked advice, and in the end he'd realized that the actions that worked for other men wouldn't work for him.

Because Raine was unlike any other woman. He'd hurt her, caused her to hurt herself and left them both extremely insecure where love was concerned. And to be honest, neither of them had started out believing that love was real.

But the pain in his heart, the gut-clenching fear he felt when he thought of Raine never forgiving him, was real. He settled her in the middle of the mattress.

"What are you doing now?" she asked. Her lips were swollen, her eyes slumberous, and he knew that his making love to her had reminded her of the good things between them.

He took the large canvas bag from the corner. A warm breeze stirred through the open tent flap. On the silk pillows, she shifted onto her side, holding her head up with her hand, her thick hair hanging in waves over her shoulders.

He cleared his throat. He tried to read her eyes to see what she felt at seeing him, but he couldn't read any emotion there.

"What's in the bag?"

"A surprise."

"I hope it isn't anything else kinky. You've worn me out."

"Have I?"

"Yes."

"I'm sorry, Raine. I want you to know that." He knew she understood his meaning.

"Me, too. I should never have tried to play you the way I did. All my life I've hated my dad for doing just that sort of thing."

"I don't think you played either of us."

She took a deep breath. "You might be right. I kept pretending I was only letting you think I was falling for you, but that wasn't true."

He leaned forward and captured her hands. "I'm glad to hear that."

She smiled. "You would be."

Her smile faded as she continued. "My life is a mess, but I realized that my own actions made it this way. It had nothing to do with you, no matter how much I wanted to blame you. I realized I took the risk with my career, the risk with my heart. And I…I think I would again."

He pulled her to him, kissed her hard and deep. "Me, too."

"So what's in the bag?" she asked.

"Apology gifts."

"Flowers and chocolate à la every romantic leading man."

"You know me well…but I'm trying to be more with you, Raine."

"You don't have to try so hard. You are more. I was teasing you."

"I know. But I really spent the last few days going over movies and television shows in my head, trying to figure out which guy to be. But in the end I realized you'd never pretended to be anyone else with me— even when you were trying to."

"I used to be much better at the con."

"Maybe, or maybe I was the first person you cared about."

"Maybe you were, Scott. That's why it hurt so much when I tried to leave."

"Tried to?"

"Well, I'm an out-of-work director. I can't go too far."

"I fixed things with Joel. Stevie and I both took the blame for what happened."

"I'm not blameless. I signed a contract and then I fraternized with one of the players."

"I'm so glad you did, Raine."

He realized that they both were in better places today than they were a few nights ago. He reached into his bag and brought out a small box.

He handed it to her. "Raine, I really love you. I'm not sure you're ready to hear that but it's the truth."

She took the package from him but set it on the pillow without opening it. Instead she cupped his face in her hands. "I love you, too. More than I thought I could. And these last few days apart have convinced me that what I'm feeling is real. Not an illusion I was trying desperately to believe."

She kissed him. Her lips were soft and tender on his. A slow embrace that promised a lifetime together. A life of taking the biggest gamble of all—marriage, children and family. But with Scott by her side those things seemed like a dream come true.

* * * * *

*Turn the page for an exclusive sneak peek
at the provocative and scandalous conclusion
to Katherine Garbera's sexy miniseries*
WHAT HAPPENS IN VEGAS…
THEIR MILLION-DOLLAR NIGHT
Available April 2006 at your favorite retail outlet.

"Roxy, this is Max Williams. Max, Roxy O'Malley. She'll be your hostess in the casino during your stay."

At Hayden's introduction, Max reached out automatically to take the woman's hand and forced his genial smile back onto his face. He'd been told by his second stepmother, Andrea, that he had the sweetest smile. Duke, his right-hand man, assured him that was not the case unless one was blind. There were too many teeth in Max's smile to miss the resemblance to a shark. But then, Duke wasn't a woman.

"Pleasure," he said. But the rest of his words stuck in his throat. Her hand was smooth and cold in his. And when he glanced into her eyes he saw how nervous she was. She was stunningly beautiful, and her body was built to make a man think of long nights and slow loving.

He held her hand longer than he knew was polite, rubbing his thumb over the back of her knuckles to warm them, until a faint blush stole over her cheeks.

"Nice to meet you, Mr. Williams."

"Call me Max."

"Max. I'm Roxy."

"I'll leave you two to it, then," Hayden said, and left.

She tugged on her hand and he let her go. "Your luggage is being taken up to your suite. Do you want to stop up there first or head straight to the casino?"

"I want…" *you,* he thought. But he knew better than to say it. He didn't understand it, this wild attraction to her. And it was wild. He didn't do lust at first sight. He had never had any problems controlling his reactions to any woman. Why her?

"Yes?"

"To go to the casino," he said at last. Other than sitting in the boardroom and negotiating a takeover there was nothing else he liked as much as playing the odds at the poker table.

She smiled at him. "Then let's go play."

"What do you think my game is?"

"Poker. And it's been your game long before the current Texas hold 'em craze that's sweeping America."

He was surprised she'd guessed it. But then he knew better than to judge a book by its cover. How many times had he been mistaken for a rich brat of a man who never worked a day in his life? Okay, not often, but it had happened.

"Don't be impressed. I read your file before you arrived. You won close to $50,000 last time you were at the poker tables."

"What else did you read about me?" he asked, wondering what was in his file. He wasn't concerned. Hayden kept stats on all the high rollers who came into the casino. Even his friends.

She tipped her head to the side, and her long hair brushed against her shoulders. He wondered if it was as soft and silky as it looked. "I can't tell you that. You'd know all my secrets for doing my job."

He caught her hand and pulled her to a stop. Damn, she had the softest skin he'd ever touched. "All of them? I doubt that. I'd only know the ones about myself. And technically, those aren't yours."

He was flirting, and he hadn't done that in a long time. The fatigue that had dogged him for the past few weeks melted away when she smiled and slipped her arm through his, leading him into the poshest section of the casino. The dinging bells and whistles of the main casino floor faded as they stepped into the high-stakes poker room.

She paused in the doorway, and Max realized that she must be new to the VIP hostess thing because she pulled them into a quiet corner instead of urging him to the table. If he wasn't already enamored with her, that would have done it. Because for the first time in a long time a woman was seeing Max Williams the man and not the bottomless bank account.

"Do you really want to know my secrets?" she asked, her voice dipping low and sounding sensual, husky.

Yes, he thought, but didn't say it out loud. He didn't know why he was reacting so strongly to her, but he knew he wasn't himself and he needed to get back on track. He wasn't looking for another affair. In fact, with the scrutiny he and his company were under right now, he couldn't afford any relationship that might make the tabloids. Right now he needed to just play.

When he said nothing, she flushed and moved away from him. "Sorry if that was too personal. Let's get you to a table and I'll bring you your favorite drink."

She started to walk away, and he almost let her but didn't. He stopped her with his fingers on her shoulder. She glanced back at him and he saw that damned vulnerability in her eyes again. "I do want to know your secrets, Roxy."

He walked past her and seated himself at a table with a few familiar faces. But instead of concentrating on the cards and the game, in his mind he saw only the surprise in Roxy's blue eyes.

It's a
SUMMER OF SECRETS

Expecting
Lonergan's Baby

(#1719)

by
MAUREEN CHILD

He'd returned only for the summer...until a
passionate encounter with a sensual stranger
has this Lonergan bachelor contemplating
forever...and fatherhood.

**Don't miss the SUMMER OF SECRETS trilogy,
beginning in April from Silhouette Desire.**

On sale April 2006
Available at your favorite retail outlet!

Visit Silhouette Books at www.eHarlequin.com SDELB0406

Baby, I'm Yours

by

CATHERINE MANN

(SD #1721)

Their affair was supposed to last
only a weekend. But an unexpected
pregnancy changed everything!

**Don't miss
RITA® Award-winning author
Catherine Mann's
Silhouette Desire debut.**

On Sale April 2006

Available at your favorite retail outlet!

Visit Silhouette Books at www.eHarlequin.com SDBIY0406

If you enjoyed what you just read,
then we've got an offer you can't resist!

Take 2 bestselling love stories FREE!

Plus get a FREE surprise gift!

Clip this page and mail it to Silhouette Reader Service™

IN U.S.A.	IN CANADA
3010 Walden Ave.	P.O. Box 609
P.O. Box 1867	Fort Erie, Ontario
Buffalo, N.Y. 14240-1867	L2A 5X3

YES! Please send me 2 free Silhouette Desire® novels and my free surprise gift. After receiving them, if I don't wish to receive anymore, I can return the shipping statement marked cancel. If I don't cancel, I will receive 6 brand-new novels every month, before they're available in stores! In the U.S.A., bill me at the bargain price of $3.80 plus 25¢ shipping and handling per book and applicable sales tax, if any*. In Canada, bill me at the bargain price of $4.47 plus 25¢ shipping and handling per book and applicable taxes**. That's the complete price and a savings of at least 10% off the cover prices—what a great deal! I understand that accepting the 2 free books and gift places me under no obligation ever to buy any books. I can always return a shipment and cancel at any time. Even if I never buy another book from Silhouette, the 2 free books and gift are mine to keep forever.

225 SDN DZ9F
326 SDN DZ9G

Name	(PLEASE PRINT)	
Address	Apt.#	
City	State/Prov.	Zip/Postal Code

Not valid to current Silhouette Desire® subscribers.

Want to try two free books from another series?
Call 1-800-873-8635 or visit www.morefreebooks.com.

* Terms and prices subject to change without notice. Sales tax applicable in N.Y.
** Canadian residents will be charged applicable provincial taxes and GST.
 All orders subject to approval. Offer limited to one per household.
 ® are registered trademarks owned and used by the trademark owner and or its licensee.

DES04R
©2004 Harlequin Enterprises Limited

**He's proud, passionate, primal—dare
she surrender to the sheikh?**

Feel warm winds blowing through your hair
and the hot desert sun on your skin as you are transported
to exotic lands.... As the temperature rises, let yourself be
seduced by our sexy, irresistible sheikhs.

In *Traded to the Sheikh* by Emma Darcy,
Emily Ross is the prisoner of Sheikh Zageo bin
Sultan al Farrahn—he seems to think she'll
trade her body for her freedom! Emily must
prove her innocence before time runs out....

TRADED TO THE SHEIKH

on sale April 2006.

www.eHarlequin.com   HPSTS0406

THE ELLIOTTS

Mixing Business with Pleasure

The saga continues with

The Forbidden Twin

by

SUSAN CROSBY

(SD #1717)

Scarlet Elliott's secret crush is finally unveiled
as she takes the plunge and seduces her twin
sister's ex-fiancé. The relationship is forbidden,
the attraction…undeniable.

On Sale April 2006

*Available at your
favorite retail outlet.*

Visit Silhouette Books at www.eHarlequin.com SDTFT0406

COMING NEXT MONTH

SDCNM0306